BEAR!

VEL ORR

June 2014

Crystal:
Good to meet
and visit with
you at Bear Country
today! Thanks for
your interest in
my book — Hope you
like the story!
Vel
author

authorHOUSE®

AuthorHouse™
1663 Liberty Drive
Bloomington, IN 47403
www.authorhouse.com
Phone: 1-800-839-8640

Published by AuthorHouse 2/4/2013

ISBN: 978-1-4817-0911-8 (sc)
ISBN: 978-1-4817-0910-1 (hc)
ISBN: 978-1-4817-0912-5 (e)

Library of Congress Control Number: 2013901046

Editor: Joe McFarland
Transcriber: Janet Orr

This book is dedicated to
all of my loving family,
with boundless gratitude

CONTENTS

ONE

CASTING HIS GREAT HEAD from side to side, testing the wind, the giant grizzly reared up on his hind legs to his full ten-feet height. Hunting in the dark and humid night, he moved slowly down a rocky yellowpine ridge. Drops of water clung to his hide from the rain shower just finished.

Lately, the bear had been subsisting on berries and white worms from rotten logs, as was typical of his kind in late summer. Because of his huge size, however, he had special need of meat in his diet and he was searching for it. The bear was uneasy. He had heard strange noises in the afternoon that he couldn't identify and the light breeze had been wrong for detecting scent. Nevertheless, his hunger was overpowering and so he hunted.

In a grass covered valley at the foot of the mountain, ahead of the approaching bear, Rose McClendon woke from a fitful sleep. She was in an officer's tent at the uphill side of a U.S. army tent camp in the Black Hills of Dakota territory. The tent was still hot from the August heat of that day in 1873. The sound of rain on the canvas, the storm sounds of thunder and wind, and the glare of lightning woke her.

Still drowzy, Rose immediately remembered making love that afternoon with scout Jim Early. She rolled on her right side and snuggled her pillow. She could still see him splashing up on his big bay horse, Jube, when he'd found her resting alone below the camp. He had been returning from his first reconnaissance of the surrounding area. She had just bathed in the cool stream that ran down the valley - Jim called it Frenchman's Creek. Refreshed, she had wanted to talk, especially to Jim. During the course of their conversation, he had told her he had known her husband. She remembered he said that he had soldiered with her Confederate Colonel husband in the war to liberate the south. He said he had been John McClendon's executive officer - a captain. Jim told her he had seen her husband killed in battle west of Appamattox at the end of the war. John was a hero of the south, he'd said.

She had cried; he had held her. He kissed her, and she begged him to love her. They knew they were meant for each other. In their passion and wild excitement, in that wild place, the hunger dammed up inside both of them burst free. Their spirits soared as in the carefree happiness of younger days. Rose remembered the look of him - his gentle touch. Jim was so handsome in his buckskins that he wore on the trail. He was big - with hard muscles - blonde hair. Rose had watched him every day as they were crossing the hot, dusty plains, and in the evenings by the campfires. He had noticed and she had caught him looking back.

Sounds of loud arguing brought Rose back to reality. She knew Captain O'Meara, Lt. Colonel Fred Grant, and Lieutenants Turnock and Johnson were drinking and playing poker in Commanding Officer O'Meara's tent at the other end of the tent row. It was obvious Fred was liquored up and being obnoxious. Rose was ashamed to be here with the damn yankee Colonel Grant, even though he was the son of the President of the United States. She had met him at a party in St. Louis when they were both drunk. He had made this summer excursion seem exciting and she'd agreed to come along - but, he was drunk or hung over all the time and no fun to be with. If they ever got out of the territory, she'd leave the boy colonel with no regrets. She fantasized riding away with Jim. Now she knew the scout felt the same way she did.

Rose tossed in her bunk. Her head was throbbing! Damned headache! As she moved her legs, she realized her flow had started. Damn!

Getting close to the army camp, the big grizzly picked up unusual scents. The bear paused as if deciding what course to take, then continued toward the camp. He stopped frequently, sniffing the wind.

Somewhat cooler after the light rain, the air was still warm and humid as Rose stepped out of the tent carrying some clean rags.

The night was very dark with black clouds rolling overhead. Head aching, half groggy, she headed out of camp for privacy.

Straight west of the row of tents there was a small opening in the high, sheer granite wall that rose like a fort behind the tents. A small creek flowed out of the opening and down the west side of the camp past the soldiers' shelters to the main creek below. From the camp, she could not see up the draw because the opening angled to the north sharply, a fissure in the huge solid rock outcrop.

She was sure the sentries would not see her move across the short distance from the tent to the little draw, it was too dark and they would mostly be watching outside the camp. As she hurried, a cold wind blew on her back out of the southeast. Rose shivered.

The bear smelled blood. He picked his way purposefully now, surefooted in the dark, down the rocky mountainside.

Her foot slipped on a muddy spot near the mouth of the draw. She regained her footing and entered the opening unnoticed, rounded the corner and walked along the small stream. Walking was treacherous in the wet grass and brush so she didn't go very far. Squatting by the stream, Rose was startled by a small noise.

A flash of lightning revealed a giant grizzly bear who now had found the source of the blood scent. Paralyzed with fear at the sight of this huge, ghostly apparition whose silver-white face seemed to glow in the glare of the lightning, she was motionless in shocked disbelief. Rose's scream died in her throat as the bear attacked, breaking her neck with one powerful swing, and life left her body.

The bear started eating at her throat, then picked her up by the shoulder, dragging her body a few yards upstream, leaving a trail of blood. He stopped to feed on the body again. The night darkened and a steady, hard rain began.

Tearing off chunks with his large canine teeth and powerful jaws, the bear ate everything as he went - flesh, muscle, bone and clothing. Full for the moment, the grizzly covered the savaged remains right where it lay beside the stream, under a pile of leaves, mud and dirt. With his massive, muscular front shoulders, huge paws and long sharp claws, the grizzly easily moved the soft earth in great spurts.

He defecated on the mound to mark it for other predators as his own food supply. The bear looked around and then walked, unhurried, a few yards into the brush to lie where he could guard his kill.

Cold rain fell in sheets for hours. The small feeder stream filled to the top of its banks with wild, muddy runoff. The swift current burst the stream banks, washing away leaves and branches, even rolling fairly large rocks. The rising water engulfed the soft mound and swept Rose's remains downstream.

Hours later, the cloudburst over, the grizzly returned to the site of the kill to feed again. Enraged to find his food supply gone, the great bear seemed to go temporarily insane. Standing up, he tore at his own face with his huge forepaws causing rows of deep scratches from which his blood flowed.

Dropping to all fours, he ran around in circles crashing through the brush and running into trees, tearing up the ground and throwing small plants in all directions. His teeth snapped together in loud threatening clacks. He charged a young twelve-foot sapling and grasping the trunk between his huge jaws, uprooted it with a mighty shake of his head.

Suddenly, the bear stopped. As quickly as his agressive display began, it was as quickly over. He walked a few steps before he dropped the sapling, shook his wet hide, and then disappeared up the wet, rocky ridge leaving no trail to follow as the sky was turning light in the east. By dawn the grizzly was two miles away, moving steadily away from the army camp and its awakening inhabitants.

Grizzlies adapt their actions to circumstances they encounter as they move through their lives, never forget a learned reaction, and are always looking for food; this bear had killed and fed upon the first human he had ever encountered.

TWO

"CUHNEL, SUH." CAPTAIN O'MEARA's orderly stood outside Grant's tent at dawn.

"Mmm."

"Cap'n he say: sun comin' up, best saddle up in an hour fo' yo' hunt."

"Mmm."

"You awake, suh?"

"Get your black ass out of here, private!"

"Yes, suh!" Pvt. Josiah Briggs returned to the campfire by the C.O.'s tent to tend the big enameled coffee pot from which the tantalizing aroma of cooking coffee now rose. Jim Early walked up the hill to the campfire leading Jube, already saddled, just as Captain O'Meara appeared.

"Good morning, Jim." The captain reached for the coffee Josiah offered.

"Good morning, sir. Did you sleep through that storm?"

"First Sgt. woke me up about two or I would have. Turned in late with plenty of whiskey under my belt so I went sound asleep just as it started raining hard."

Early spit out some coffee grounds. "Some of the boys washed out down below and we had to move the tents that were too close to that little creek", Jim said. "First Sgt. said he better tell you."

"Yeah, this can be pretty violent country - so hot yesterday and I was froze stiff when I woke up." Captain O'Meara turned to his orderly. "Josiah, did you call the others?"

"Yes,suh!"

"Go saddle Star and bring her up then, and your mule. Better swing by and pick up the dried meat that cook's got ready for me ...

5

and some coffee." They would need the provisions for the elk hunt they were ready to start on. The hunt was Grant's idea and was the stated reason they were in the Black Hills. They were in the middle of the Sioux reservation which was guaranteed to the indians by their treaty with the general government. Highly irregular being here, even illegal, but the son of the President could pretty much get what he wanted. O'Meara knew there was more to it.

Josiah was already started down the hill when Colonel Grant stepped out of his tent, blinked his eyes in the strong, early sun, and called Captain O'Meara over.

"Mrs. McClendon is gone," the captain said as the two officers rejoined the scout by the fire. Both looked plenty worried. Young Grant's eyes were bloodshot and he looked scared. His presence was less than commanding this morning in the rumpled uniform he had evidently slept in and with the scraggly black beard he had let grow on this expedition. He smelled of booze and sweat, cigars and puke.

"What do you mean - gone? Where is she?" Jim was instantly alarmed.

"If I knew that, I wouldn't need to tell you, Early!" The colonel threw up his hands. "You're paid to scout. Find her."

"When did you last see her, sir?"

"Yesterday in the C.O.'s tent," Grant said.

"You mean she wasn't in your tent when you turned in last night?" Jim asked.

"I don't know." Grant turned aside.

"I'll look around," Jim had a sick feeling in his gut. "That hard rain will make it tough to find any tracks. Better call off the elk hunt, sir."

Captain O'Meara nodded. "Let's keep this quiet 'til we get to the bottom of it."

Jim led Jube to Grant's tent, studying the ground as he walked. Looking west, he noticed the draw. As he neared the creek flowing out of the draw, he saw the mud and debris scattered wide along the little stream. He also noticed a scrape where someone might have slipped and an indentation that could have been a small footprint but was now washed away beyond positive identification.

"Whoa, Jube." Jim caught the bridle with one hand and clamped down on the horse's nose with his other hand. The big bay side-stepped and tried to break away. As Jim held on with all his strength, Jube reared up, wild eyed. "Whoa, Jube, whoa," Jim soothed.

Jim led the trembling horse back away from the draw and tied him to a tree behind the officers' tents. He pulled his Spencer from the scabbard and rummaged through a saddle bag for his short-barrel Colt revolver and extra shells. His Spencer was his pride. The repeater had been extremely popular on both sides during the war and Jim had carried one at the last. He felt lucky to have one now because the general government had big financial problems after the war, the treasury was empty, and most soldiers still carried old single-shot Springfields. Even cavalry troops still had the old issue rifles.

The loaded seven-shot lever-action Spencer and the six-shot revolver made Jim feel he was ready for anything, but old habit caused him to stuff extra ammunition in his pockets. He was walking away from his supplies and didn't know what he would need or when he would again be walking up to Jube's side. Better to be safe.

Early also preferred the short Colt he carried as a personal weapon to the more cumbersome regular issue 7" barreled Colt. In fact, regular issue to scouts was also mandated by the Congress to be nickel-plated - a bad idea.

Whatever spooked Jube must be up that draw, Jim figured. "I sure as hell don't like the looks of this."

Stepping into the draw, Jim stopped. The back of his neck felt clammy as he surveyed the wanton destruction in the rain-soaked vale. He half-raised his rifle instinctively as he advanced a few steps. He saw and recognized what was left of the kill mound, blood that hadn't washed away, and a clear big track with one toe missing. He had seen an old track like that in dried out mud yesterday on recon.

"Bear!" he murmured "That big sonuvabitch ..." Jim picked up a bloody, torn piece of Rose's dress ... "killed Rose!" Jim tensed in shock and disbelief as sorrow, anger, and hate washed over him.

THREE

"EARLY, YOU LOOK LIKE a horse just kicked you in the face," Grant said as Jim returned to the C.O.'s tent. "You haven't found Rose yet? You'd better get on your horse and look around a bigger area."

The scout was stunned; he still couldn't believe Rose was gone. He leaned his rifle against the trunk of a pine. It was hard to say anything, especially to this crude young man who had spent quite a bit of time with her but who didn't know Rose at all. Grant was too self-centered to care about anyone else or anything except being on a great adventure and filling his gut with whiskey.

"Damn it, Early..."

"Jim, what is it? What's wrong?" the captain asked.

"Rose is dead, Captain. She was killed in the night by a bear. Around the corner where that creek comes through the rocks, there's blood all over and bear sign. Her body must have washed away in that flash flood. I'll ride downstream and look for her."

Grant jumped up. "We've got to get out of here without the troops realizing Rose is gone. Early, I don't want you to call unnecessary attention to this by searching for Rose's body, then bringing it into camp. We mustn't let a reb's widow become an embarrassment to the President. No, we must leave now."

"Colonel, I'm sure you're right but let's think about ... " O'Meara started to say.

Grant's eyes flashed. "This is your command, Captain, but I'm on special assignment orders to join General Custer as acting aide. These are his 7th Cavalry troops. I'm pulling rank on you here."

Grant's mouth felt dry as cotton as he tried to spit - a little spot fell by his boot. "General Custer may not be back yet from his Yellowstone campaign. He's out in Montana territory protecting railroad surveyors from Crazy Horse's Sioux. That's why we had time enough for this unofficial trip to the Black Hills while en-route to station. We can resume our march to Lincoln and no one needs to know about Rose or any damned bear."

"How'll we keep the men from realizing Rose is gone?" the captain asked. Grant shifted his weight from one leg to the other. "We'll let it be known she's sick and that's why we're changing plans and leaving. We can have the side curtains pulled on the ambulance for the trip."

"This whole thing makes me sick," Jim said. "If you do fool the troops now, how will you make them believe she's in the ambulance all the way to Lincoln?"

"We'll just take it one step at a time, Early. You just keep your mouth shut and let me run the deception."

Later, as Grant and Early carried the litter down the hillside, with an army blanket rolled up under Rose's down comforter, no one paid any particular attention as everyone else worked at breaking camp. Grant was visibly relieved as he closed the ambulance door and ordered some soldiers to strike the officers' tents and went about gathering up his gear. He worked between the troopers and the opening in the rock wall in case someone decided to look around. The men quickly did their work and returned below.

Early approached O'Meara. "Captain, you'll have no trouble getting to Ft. Lincoln from here. I'm staying to kill the bear. My scout contract will be up soon anyway. The Black Hills is Sioux reservation by treaty and if I don't stay now, I may never get another chance. Sir, I have to find Rose and kill that bear."

"I have to have you, Jim, until we get to Lincoln. If we run into hostiles, we'll need every rifle. The plains indians are on the warpath everywhere. Just leaving you here alone is leaving you to be killed. Besides, you're under my orders to perform to your contract. No, you can't stay." The Captain walked away.

Jim got his gear together for the march. He dropped his Colt back in the saddle bag and hung his loaded carbine in his saddle scabbard.

The bugler blew "boots and saddles" and the troops fell in to head downstream, back the same way they had come the day before. Early sat his horse off to one side where he was joined by the mounted officers. He watched all the U.S. branded horses go by, listening to the normal sounds of the animals, the shouted commands, the jingle and creak of bits and harness, the snap of the 7th Cavalry flag, and the rumble of the wagons as the command got under way. Somehow, it now all seemed out of place here, like an unwanted intrusion into a big, sacred church.

Early's whole body ached for Rose. Poor Rose. Jim grieved her loss and the life they might have shared together. Their love yesterday seemed to have come suddenly, but he realized there had been a solid attraction ever since they had first met. She had been so beautiful.

He joined the officers as they fell in behind the main body of troops and ahead of the mule drawn wagons and rear guard. The ambulance was right behind the officers, the first drawn conveyance in the column. "Grant can watch it right well," Jim thought.

As they moved away, Jim took one last look at the bank of Frenchman's Creek where he rode up to Rose - just yesterday! The fallen pine log that was across the stream then was gone now. The creek was now high and muddy and there was debris everywhere. As his lingering gaze came back to the stream, his sharp eyes noticed a soggy bundle in a tangle of branches and sticks caught above some willows along the opposite bank.

"Captain," Jim said softly, "I just saw Rose's body in the creek. I'm going to ride off up the hill and scout the area, then I'll circle back when the train is out of sight and bury her. I'll join up with you again before you get out of the hills."

"Early, if you don't come back, I'll personally run you down and you'll rot in an army stockade for breaking your contract," O'Meara snarled quietly.

Jim touched Jube's flank with his heel and his neck with the right rein and moved off up the hill without answering.

FOUR

LATER, AFTER WRAPPING ROSE'S remains in his poncho, Early placed her body in a natural depression next to a caved off bank on the hillside above the stream. Jim easily caved the soft, black soil down on her body with his skinning knife and a piece of tree branch.

When the site was leveled off and there were several feet of earth covering her in the grave, he carried and rolled big rocks to make a mound over the spot.

Finished, he prayed in his private grief, oblivious to all about him. Jim swore to all that is sacred and to Rose's memory that he would come back to kill the bear.

Hours had passed since he rode away from the troops. He saddled his horse again and led him down to the creek. The water had cleared up some and was lower now. As Jube drank noisily, Jim noticed a bright glint at the edge of the creek in the water. He picked up a small gold nugget as big as his little finger nail. Jim rubbed it between his thumb and forefinger and dropped it in his pocket.

Jim washed his hands and face in the cold water and then lay flat on the bank and put his face in the water, rinsing out the taste of vomit from when he had moved Rose's body. As he raised his head out of the creek, he had a momentary sensation of danger just as a rifle barrel cracked him behind the left ear and he sagged unconscious, face down in the stream.

A blue-sleeved arm with three stripes reached down and pulled Jim out of the creek. "There, that'll hold ya Johnny Reb. Any damn fool who'd call his horse Jube is braggin' he's a Lee man. I knew about ya fer a long time, just waitin' fer the right time. I'd let ya drown but the Cap'n's lookin' fer me to bring ya back. Be better if ya was alive. I can wait."

The burly soldier threw the scout across Jube's saddle like a sack of spuds. Jube pranced sideways as creek water poured out of Jim's mouth and nose. "Whoa, ya hammerhead," the sergeant grabbed Jube's bridle and jerked him back. Jim shuddered and moaned.

"There, ya'll be breathin' alright again, Reb."

Tying Jim's hands to a stirrup, the soldier passed the rope under Jube's belly, tied the other end to Jim's ankles, and cinched it tight to keep Jim from falling off. Jube jumped and kicked as the rough rope sawed on his belly. "Whoa, you sonuvabitch." The sergeant grabbed Jube's reins, swung up on his own mount and headed downstream.

When Jim came to, his head throbbed. Brush slapped his face and legs as he bounced along tied to Jube's back. Turning his face to the front, he recognized the heavy, muscular back of Sgt. Mueller, U.S.A. "What the hell?"

"Oh, ya finally come 'round, did ya? We're gettin' close ta catchin' up with the troop."

Jim groaned. Pain bounced around in his head in lightning stabs.

"Cap'n told me ta look for ya around last night's camp. He said if I found ya ta make sure ya come back with me, by force if necessary, as he said. I figured I didn't want no trouble, so I'm bringing ya back the easiest way I know how."

They rode by a limestone cliff face. An indian jumped from hiding on a ledge of the cliff, landing partly on the sergeant and partly on his horse. The horse stumbled, then bolted toward the creek. Jube's thin leather reins snapped in two as Jube reared.

"Let's go, Jube." Jim drummed on Jube's side with his bound hands. Jube raced flat out, ears laid back, at a full gallop. Jim passed out again from the pounding his body was taking.

When he woke up this time he was on his back on the ground looking up at familiar army faces. Jube had reached the troop.

"Cheyennes, Captain," Jim said. "They're close. I saw paint and a crow feather on the buck that jumped Mueller." Then, he passed out.

In a few minutes, Jim was awake again. "Take a look, Jim." O'Meara handed his field glass to the scout. Early glassed the mountainside above their hastily prepared fortification. Teamsters led spare mules inside the defense circle. Shots rang out. The mules were killed and dropped around the perimeter for breastworks. Soldiers took up defensive positions.

"Looks like Whirlwind Horse's dog soldiers, sir," Jim said. "They're supposed to be around here this summer. Probably were hunting buffalo and came upon us by chance but they're all painted up and stripped down for battle."

"Isn't Whirlwind Horse a Southern Cheyenne? What the hell is he doing in Dakota?" Grant asked.

"Whirlwind Horse's people were with old Black Kettle at Sand Creek in Colorado in '64, Colonel. Chivington's irregulars wiped out his family along with about 150 other women and children. Only a few Cheyenne men were killed, the old and the very young, because most of the men were off hunting. Since he came north, he's formed up a band of young hotheads, a fairly large camp. They're a mixture of Southern and Northern Cheyenne's with maybe a few Sioux, and they'd be spoiling to kill us all."

"How do you know that's who they are, anyway?" Grant demanded.

"I said it looks like them. Sioux on the warpath wear eagle feathers, a lot of them wear war bonnets. These are wearing single crow feathers and the ones I can see looking us over, three or four in a small clearing high on the mountain, have red streamers on their war lances. That's supposed to be them ... wait a minute ... I'm sure the one who just rode up is Whirlwind Horse. Red war-paint all over him and he's a bull of a man. He's learned a lot since Sand Creek. We'll have one hell of a fight."

"Shoot the sonuvabitch," Grant said.

"Too far now but he'll give you a better chance, Colonel, they'll be down here with us soon enough." Jim handed the glass to Capt. O'Meara. The indians disappeared on the mountain.

FIVE

As HE LED THEM into the timber, high on the mountain, Whirlwind Horse scolded his young braves for showing themselves to the pony soldiers.

Brilliant red paint glowing on his very dark, broad face, Whirlwind Horse was a terror to his enemies in battle. A fierce giant, veteran of many running battles with the bluecoats, he was a powerful man commanding the respect of his men as well as their enemies. With his natural savvy of tactics and maneuvers, the dog soldiers usually ended up whipping the pony soldiers in hit and run fights. Thick, black hair fell loose to his broad shoulders. His arms and legs heavily muscled, his waist slim, he was a born warrior who loved war. His medicine was so powerful, not only did he return unharmed time after time, but his protection seemed also to shield those who rode at his side. Whirlwind Horse believed the life color to be his special medicine. Yes, the color red preserves the life of he who wears it. That's why his dog soldiers all carried medicine lances with bright red buckskin wrappings and streamers. Whirlwind Horse always painted red circles around the eyes of his own white pony when preparing for battle. Together, they had survived many battles.

Owl Woman took the lead rope of his pony as the war chief jumped to the ground. Some Cheyenne women had come along on the hunting party to take care of the buffalo hides, meat, and daily camp life. Now, they would follow the war party to give a hand.

Whirlwind looked with satisfaction at his band of several hundred battle-tested, practiced horsemen as he rejoined them. Cheyenne warriors believed war to be noble. Battle gave them

17

pleasure and earned them respect and admiration. They were excited now, anxious for revenge on these white soldiers.

The Cheyenne and the Arapaho, their nations too small for separate treaties, had smoked the war pipe with their Sioux brothers all swearing vengeance on the whites. By mutual consent, they shared ranges that were treated to the Sioux, like the western Dakota plains. The Sioux had always been enemies of the whites and welcomed these good warriors as allies.

Whirlwind's band was a strong Cheyenne camp. Fierce fighters, they were a soldier society of their tribe. The best warriors of the plains indians, the Cheyenne took excessive risks in battle and lost many men in proportion to their numbers.

Whirlwind Horse wished his braves all carried modern repeating rifles like his own. He called his Henry "yellow boy" because the receiver was made of brass and this one was decorated for indian trade with a brass butt plate and brass tacks design on the stock. He was a good shot with his fast-talkin' gun. His men, however, had a few rifles but not much ammunition for them. All were experienced and competent with bows and arrows and lances, and were deadly at close range from horseback with any weapon.

In a large clearing on top of the mountain, above and out of sight of the cavalry company, Whirlwind called his people to council to smoke the war pipe. Quickly assembled, the familiar faces of Tall Bear, Eagle-Who-Attacks, Bull Buffalo, Antelope Tail, Hoop, and Spotted Horse ringed the council fire and the men slowly passed the pipe.

A fiercely painted dog soldier rode up to the council at a gallop, pulling up just a few feet short of the seated leaders. A cloud of dust fell over the others as he who now called himself Grey Blanket slid to the ground. His favorite war pony pawed and reared before backing away to stand waiting.

They made room for Grey Blanket. His eyes flashing, he reached for his turn at the pipe. Black Bear and Little Horse, Oglalla Sioux brothers who were members of the dog soldiers; Swift Dog, and Left Hand joined the circle to round out the leaders' council. As they smoked, hundreds of warriors gathered.

Four braves squatted around a large drum and started pounding the taut surface of the stretched buffalo hide. The primitive beat swelled. A war dance began and the frenzied warriors danced, sometimes falling out to rest before returning to dance again.

Off to one side, alone, the old medicine man White Bull prayed to the Great Medicine Man for swift victory to overcome the yellow-leg soldiers. His unearthly chant rang out eerily against the pines and rocks. The yips and war cries of the dancing indians set a wild, primitive scene.

Each war chief, in turn, smoked and spoke for making war against the pony soldiers to teach the white men to stay out of the sacred Paha Sapa and these hunting grounds.

At last, Whirlwind Horse spoke. "I swear to fight to the death the bluecoats who dare to come to my country. To my sacred Paha Sapa they come. We must not let them get away. The Great Spirit will guide and protect us and the great medicine of the red lance will keep us safe."

"If any of us is impure, if I am impure and die, we go with great honor if we die defending our people and this land. This land was the land of our fathers and their fathers and we were here long before the white man came - even before the Sioux came here."

"This is our hunting ground by treaty, and Paha Sapa is the center of the universe where the hoop of the world bends to the four directions. Now, the words of the white dogs blow away in the wind and they come to steal our land."

"We must show the enemy we will fight to the death to keep our land and our buffalo. We have learned his tricks from his peace councils, from our raiding party battles, and from our fight to protect the people ever since they slaughtered our women and children at Sand Creek. There can be no peace now. My heart is hard against the bluecoats and all the whites. Today, all of them who are here must die."

Whirlwind Horse jumped upright, raised his war lance with a mighty lunge, and let out a blood-curdling war cry. All the warriors mounted with a loud cry and headed for battle. Now the old medicine man's continuing wail was the only sound except the wind in the trees in the quiet forest. The warriors rode silently so the pony soldiers would not know when they would attack.

SIX

"Damn me! Thaze a thousand of them red devils up there! Sure and we'll be slaughtered here in this godforsaken wilderness!" whispered Private Patrick Murphy as the war dance started on the mountain above, and the shrieks and howls were carried plainly on the light hot wind.

"Why we pinned down on this damned bare knob waitin' ta be killed?" Private Alexander Atwood asked. "Save a bullet fer yerself, Pat, less ya wanna be scalped alive er taken priz'ner by injuns." Atwood shuddered.

Captain O'Meara had picked his spot in a hurry, knowing the Cheyenne were painted for war and that his command would be attacked at any time. He knew it was useless to try to run. The indians on their fast ponies could overtake at will the slower army column with its wagons and mules. The small column was alone - too far from any help.

The army fortification had been hastily placed on a bare foothill on the east slope of the Black Hills. They were below the timberline on the mountain, but above the prairie that lay east to the horizon of the sunrise. The foothill was actually covered with high grasses and loose rock. The position commanded a good field of fire in all directions which afforded the troop the best available place to defend themselves against what might be a superior force attacking. Captain O'Meara worried about the west approach from the mountain above them where Whirlwind Horse's warriors could attack downhill. Still, there was a hundred yards of open hillside that the hostiles had to cross to carry out their assault.

Troops were bringing the last of their wagons up the gradual slope of the north side which afforded easy accessibility. Here

21

again, the soldiers could pick off riders before they could breach the defense. There were a few knee-high pines on the north side widely spaced, none big enough to hide the attackers. The east side hill was steeper with a narrow, brushy and rocky ravine running down to the prairie. Most of the side towards the prairie was caved off, cliff-like and inaccessible. The steep slope of the south side was studded with huge boulders. A rim of mature pines grew above that slope along the entire south side of the army position.

O'Meara's men were arranged in a circle on the flat grassy top, facing out, with rifle rests made up of whatever the men could find - dead mules or rocks, sometimes a saddle. Larger objects would serve to shield the troops from enemy sight and give the soldiers some protection. His sixty disciplined men should be able to hold off the attack and kill enough savages so they would lose interest and withdraw from the field.

In the center of the troop's enclosure, lined up from east to west were all their wagons and conveyances. The tallest was the ambulance which was about dead center in the ringed defense. O'Meara had a wagon load of ammunition of various sizes that he was delivering to Ft. Lincoln, but no spare weapons.

He also had his cook's wagons and supplies with jerked buffalo and antelope they had gathered as they had come across the prairie to the Black Hills only days ago. Their water kegs were full from camp last night.

Captain O'Meara worked his way around his defenses, reassuring his men. He had placed his best shooters on the west, under Lt. Turnock, armed with the half dozen fast-firing carbines he had been able to acquire for his command. These were 7-shot, lever action rifles that could make it hot for anyone coming in on that side. Jim Early and Colonel Grant were at the center of the north edge, both armed with their own Spencers and pistols. Murphy and Atwood were at the east end with their single-shot Springfields laid over dead mules. They were covering the relatively less vulnerable access. The Captain had ordered all men to be supplied with plenty of ammunition from the ammo wagon and all of them had some rations and water at their side.

"Captain, suh, Cap'n! Scout say come take a look by the crick!"

Josiah seemed calm but there was urgency in his voice. O'Meara, with Josiah at his heels, joined Early and Grant.

"Look toward where we came out of Frenchman's Creek, Captain. Looks like a man there."

O'Meara pulled his field glass. "Looks like a trooper - it's Sgt. Mueller and he's down."

As the screams and drum beat continued above them, O'Meara sent out Sgt. Dalton and two privates on foot to bring Mueller in. They ran down the hill and across the flat. Mueller was unconscious and bloody but alive. His saddled horse stood nearby. The men loaded Mueller on his saddle and, holding him in place, hurried back up the hill to safety without incident. Mueller stirred but did not revive. Several men knelt to tend him.

A private led Mueller's horse outside the defense perimeter, put the reins over the saddle, pulled the bit out of his mouth, and slapped his rear haunch. The horse bolted and, still saddled and bridled, ran around the hill to the other horses in the corral below the cliff. A single line of lasso ropes tied to various small pines encircled the horses.

Uneasy in their enclosure, the horses were moving around a bit, but they weren't greatly agitated. They were one more level below the troops. The extra distance soaked up the noise of the war dance. Mueller's horse stood by the rope fence, patiently eating grass.

The noise from the indian camp got louder, with more screams and war cries from the excited dancers. The afternoon hours passed slowly for the cavalry troops. Many of the edgy defenders were afraid.

Lt. Colonel Grant tried to steady himself with whiskey. After about an hour and a half of listening to the distant war dance, Grant vomited over the dead mule breastwork and passed out, his face very pale. Another spasm in his throat forced puke out of the corner of his mouth that dribbled on his tunic. Grant sighed and slumped unconscious.

Captain O'Meara quietly set Josiah up with a Springfield and ammunition, to bolster the defense near Grant but with another soldier in between them. If Grant woke up in the heat of battle, O'Meara didn't want Grant to harm his orderly.

When the war dance stopped after what seemed like an eternity of waiting, loud indian yells swelled and then went silent. The only sound on the breeze was the thin, eerie wail of the old medicine man praying.

By this time, Murphy had mumbled his Catholic prayers many times. Both Murphy and Atwood were older teamsters with many years in the army, but neither had ever faced the danger of battle before. They were both petrified with fear. Other men squirmed, their eyes watered from looking over their rifle barrels for so long. They talked to each other in whispers.

White Bull kept praying for about another half hour, then the only sound was the sigh of the pine branches moving in the light wind. Whirlwind Horse was in position, hidden in the trees above the fortification, ready to strike.

The excited warriors were eager to wipe out the troop and after waiting a short while in dead silence while the chief looked over the army position, Grey Blanket could stand it no longer. Carrying his red-streamered lance, he kneed his pony's ribs with repeated sharp jabs and rode at a gallop straight for the soldiers' line. He was close before the troops realized the wait was over. As the first shot rang out, Grey Blanket turned, yipping and yelling and rode the length of the north side of the position. A ragged volley chased him but there were no hits.

As Grey Blanket neared the east end, he rode close to the line and speared the campaign hat off Murphy's head with his lance and rode down the draw to the plain below. As he turned along the cliff face, he raced up to the horse herd with sharp cries and stampeded them over their rope corral. He galloped most of them west and up a valley toward the sacred mountains. Grey Blanket's magnificent ride would be much honored in the Cheyenne lodges and at pow wows without count.

When Grey Blanket had neared the middle of the north line, holding the attention of the defenders, Whirlwind Horse and his fighting dog soldiers erupted from the timber. They followed Grey Blanket's path, as hundreds poured into the fray. The huge force flowed past the west end and along the north side in wave after wave.

Rattled, but now not surprised, O'Meara's 7th Cavalry company settled down to kill indians. Hundreds of mounted Cheyenne advanced screaming at a gallop - the soldiers had plenty of targets. Some warriors rode upright on their ponies showing contempt for the yellow-legs fire power, and demonstrating unshakeable belief in their protective medicine.

Whirlwind Horse and most of his followers, however, slid forward on their mount, hooked their right leg over their pony's back, grabbed a handful of mane with one hand, and swung down to look and fire under the horse's neck.

Whirlwind Horse drew first blood. When an excited trooper raised up to get a better shot as the horde descended, Whirlwind's Henry barked. One of the soldiers' repeating carbines lay under the dead body, silenced for the rest of this attack.

The Sioux, Little Horse, got off a fire arrow in the early minutes which struck the company's ambulance. Little Horse was immediately shot dead. Unnoticed in the heat of battle, the painted wood blazed quickly.

A dying indian screamed, shot as he tried to breech the defense line on the north. His scream was piercing and sounded like a woman's scream. Some soldiers thought it must be Rose and instinctively glanced at the ambulance which was by then engulfed in flames.

Grant's deception was done. The command thought Rose McClendon died here. Fred Grant, awake now, fired drunkenly at the mass of indians and horses sweeping past.

The entrenched troops took a toll, mostly the easy targets sitting their ponies as they charged. Others shot ponies and then their riders when the warrior jumped clear of the falling animal. Some indians whose ponies were shot dropped behind their dead horse, then crawled and ran down the north slope to be picked up below by a comrade - saved by their powerful medicine. Withering fire from the troops turned aside the Cheyenne attack.

Thirty five warriors and many ponies lay dead on the slopes around the fortification as the indians withdrew, unable to overwhelm the position. The assault had resulted in ten dead in the cavalry ranks - heavy casualties for the small troop.

SEVEN

WHEN THE BLUNTED ATTACK ended, the Cheyenne disappeared back into the pines. The sun went down and a mostly cloudy sky brought early darkness to the plains.

Jim Early got up, stretched, and walked a little to shake off the stiffness and aches caused by the cramped positions of battle. He saw that everyone else was also moving around some, while keeping an eye outside the enclosure. Jim tended a wounded man. Others moved bodies off the line and covered them with blankets under the trees at the south edge of the fortification. Second Lieutenant Johnson had been one of the first killed in the attack.

Captain O'Meara deployed a scattering of men around his perimeter, allowing others to sleep a few hours before they took their turns at the line positions. A latrine was dug above the cliff.

Soldiers busied themselves eating, improving battle positions and making ready battle gear for the next attack if the indians returned, and then tried to rest. Lt. Colonel Grant slept fitfully at his position. There was an ominous foreboding of impending disaster throughout the camp.

Atwood and Murphy stayed at their posts at the east end of the defense, talking in whispers.

"Wha'ud ya think o' slippin' away in the dark an' makin' fer the river, Alex?" asked Murphy.

"That's desertion, Pat."

"Be damned, I'd sooner be a live deserter than a dead hero. Damn me, if we stay here we'll die with the rest. There ain't no way outa here, I don't care what the Cap'n says. We can't hold out against that damn many injuns too long."

"If'n we leave now, ain't no one'll notice us and the redskins'r

27

above us in the timber. Let's crawl down this gulley ta the east 'n make tracks 'cross the prairie. Ever damn man for his self as I see it, Alex."

"Pat, I'm scared ta stay and scared ta move. Maybe we're safer here with guns'n ammo an' food'n water."

"Ya wanna be scalped? ... alive? Damn me, I'm gonna try it whether ya come er not. That devil spearin' my hat taday - he knows I'm here."

"Let's wait 'til later when more a the boys are sleepin' - we'll have a better chance ta get away if you're gonna do it."

"Sure, and yew try to sleep a while. I'll watch first, Alex."

Captain O'Meara showed up out of the dark checking the positions. "Keep a sharp eye, men," he whispered as he passed along to the next position.

"Yes, sur." Murphy said.

Hours later, Murphy and Atwood crawled over their dead mule breastworks and slipped out of the quiet camp, down the gulley as planned. Unnoticed by the command, they disappeared from sight and sound of the comrades they were leaving behind. Murphy stubbed his boot on a small rock, kicking it loose. The rock rolled ahead and the men froze in fear. When there was no apparent alarm after a few minutes, the pair resumed their descent, more carefully than ever. Single file, they passed the bush where Tall Bear was hiding.

Tall Bear waited, motionless and scarcely breathing, until the two teamsters were well past him, then he silently crept up behind the rear man. With Tall Bear's hand over his mouth and his throat deftly cut, Private Alexander Atwood died with a surprised look on his face. The trooper's eyes bulged above Tall Bear's hand. The indian restrained Atwood's body from thrashing about.

"Begorra, Alec, be quiet! Watch yer step! It's dark but we're not clear a the post yet. Damn me, if they hear us, they'll come after us and shoot us for damn deserters!"

"Alex, catch up, we're too far apart." Murphy tried to see behind him to catch sight of Atwood. As he paused, he looked in front of him to the east again. Tall Bear closed in silently and cut his throat just as he had Atwood's.

Out of breath now, Tall Bear squatted in the gulley to regain his strength and composure. Then, he scalped both soldiers and crawled up to the top of the gulley to the very edge of the army defense perimeter. Under cover of darkness, with a very loud war whoop, Tall Bear threw the scalps into the enclosure and immediately dropped to the ground. Scattered shots rang out in his direction as Tall Bear skidded down the gulley, rolling and jumping until he reached the plain below. He scurried around the south end of the promontory and escaped west toward where Grey Blanket had driven the U.S. horses. The troops had little chance to hit Tall Bear. They fired in vain down the gulley in pitch darkness, unable to see what they were shooting at.

Some soldiers followed the sounds of Tall Bear's hurried descent down the draw, firing random shots until they stumbled on the troopers' bodies. In confusion, they fired a few more shots, then carried the dead men back up to their camp.

No more of Captain O'Meara's company would risk going over the hill to desert his command. All were impressed with the indians' fighting ability and afraid to test indian strategy in less force than company strength. All were committed to their positions until the end of the engagement.

EIGHT

LISTENING TO TALL BEAR'S account of his exploit, Whirlwind Horse thought of a plan to attack the yellowlegs yet again this night. In council on the mountain top, Whirlwind explained his strategy to his battle leaders as they passed the war pipe around the council fire.

"We are close to the pony soldiers here and can reach them quickly. They did not chase Tall Bear. They are afraid and do not leave their fort. We must go to them."

"When the sun is high their rifles are too strong for us to ride over. We must go now with no moon or stars to show us to them. I say we send Hoop and as many warriors as you can count on one hand to get into the white man's circle from the side."

"They must think this is our attack." Whirlwind Horse thoughtfully puffed on the war pipe.

"When they are busy with Hoop, we will ride down the mountain with our attack. We will enter their fort and kill them with axes in close battle because we can't see to shoot. The soldiers will be blind to us. We are many and they are few. We are on horses and they are in holes. We will kill them all."

Because Whirlwind's afternoon attack the day before had not resulted in death to all the soldiers and had resulted in the deaths of so many Cheyenne and Sioux brothers, several in the council felt they should listen to another leader and not follow Whirlwind Horse and his plans.

Bull Buffalo wanted to cover himself with glory by leading the deciding attack. He argued that they must not attack "like a pack of cowardly coyotes in the night" but should lay siege to the white

31

man and wait in safety until the enemy did something foolish and exposed themselves to the waiting indians.

Hot-headed Spotted Horse quickly sided with Bull Buffalo. Others grunted as Spotted Horse spoke, but Whirlwind Horse spoke to Hoop. Hoping to show his bravery to Moon Star's father, Hoop agreed to lead the diversion.

Hoop was young but sat in the leader's council because of his bravery and leadership shown in raiding parties. He was eager to share in the personal glory now shown Grey Blanket and Tall Bear. Whirlwind Horse pulled himself up to his imposing full stature, arguing forcefully in the flickering firelight. Whirlwind Horse had led his people against the whites in many raids and was a survivor of the Colorado and Kansas purges of the southern Cheyenne.

Whirlwind was strong, his bravery and his hatred of white soldiers unquestioned, and his great medicine was thought to be protection even for his comrades in battle. Whirlwind Horse prevailed and the dog soldiers rode to set the trap.

Hoop picked a half dozen warriors to accompany him and they rode down the southwest side of the mountain to the plain below. They would circle in from the south as Whirlwind Horse's main force got into position west of the troop's fortification in the same assembly area they had used in the first attack.

Dark of night still held, but cloud cover in the east was breaking up as Hoop's party started up the south slope on foot, moving from boulder to boulder. The moon broke from the clouds, bathing the prairie and the mountain in sudden moonlight.

Jim Early, the seasoned war veteran and sharpshooter, was pulling duty on the south defense perimeter with his repeater Spencer laid across a boulder. The breaking moonlight revealed an indian between boulders about half way up the hill below him.

Early dropped him with a quick reaction shot and the indian lay kicking on the hillside. "Good shot" thought Jim. Then he was very busy shooting as the indians below scurried to pick up the fallen warrior. Jim shot two more, pinning the attack party down behind boulders. Captain O'Meara was suddenly at his elbow placing two more shooters next to Jim.

How does it look, Jim?" O'Meara asked.

"Small party, Captain. If the moon hadn't come out, they would have probably been on top of me in the dark. We got lucky here. I can see beyond this group and there's no more behind them. This hillside is a poor access, they have to be on foot. This just can't be a major attack."

"We're alerted all around - everyone's awake" O'Meara said. "Keep a sharp eye. I think you're right, this is diversionary. The moonlight's in our favor. They make good targets and since we're under cover and in shadows, we're not. I say, let 'em come. I'm sure glad you were here with that carbine! How many did you get?"

"Hit three, I think - pretty good hits," Jim answered.

Hoop's party stayed down as the moonlight brightened into dawn. At daylight, Early could see two bodies below him. The Cheyenne prepared to stay put until the next darkness. Hoop and three others of his party were not hurt, two were dead, and another was dying behind a rock.

Five warriors took positions along the tree line above the troops to occasionally fire into the army group throughout the day. The rest of the second day of siege passed with the cavalry pinned down by sniper fire and Hoop's party pinned down in an exposed area. No casualties were inflicted on either side.

The troops were reasonably comfortable with food and water and ammunition replenished during the dark of the night before. It was oppressively hot now with no breeze for relief. Big, black, horse flies were constantly stinging the back of someone's neck or hand. No one could safely move to the latrine. At least, no one wanted to be shot with his pants down, so small holes were dug in place as needed. Whirlwind Horse had withdrawn his force to the mountain top.

Whirlwind Horse had failed again to overcome the cavalry position. Bull Buffalo's plan of siege was actually now in practice, at least at the moment. The leaders gathered together for hours on the mountain top unable to decide on strategy or whom to follow into battle or even whether to stay or withdraw from the field.

Everyone argued in the August heat. Antelope Tail spoke for leaving the army troops to allow them to go. He argued, but without support in the council, that the army had learned a lesson here and wouldn't come back if the Cheyenne allowed them to go away.

Bull Buffalo and Spotted Horse gained support for their siege plan. Whirlwind Horse favored keeping the pony soldiers at bay, increasing pressure with sniper fire until conditions were good for an all out attack. No agreement could be reached. Hot and tired, the indians left the council, one at a time, until there was no one to argue. No plan was formed.

At dark, the warrior snipers came into the camp. Several more rode out to watch the soldier encampment but confusion about how to proceed prevented Whirlwind from taking any strong action against the trapped soldiers. The Cheyenne didn't like to fight at night. Their acceptance of Whirlwind's plan the first night was testimony to their belief in his ability, flying in the face, as it did, of their usual feelings.

Hoop and his three remaining warriors came in after dark and joined Whirlwind Horse at his sleeping space to tell him about the fate of their sortie. Sudden moonlight had destroyed the entire battle plan.

Whirlwind Horse must act soon with a plan that would not fail or the bluecoat soldiers would win the fight because the Cheyenne were losing interest going into the third day. Some of his people were already disappearing into Paha Sapa or riding away to the north. Most of the dog soldiers were fierce in battle in the heat of passion, but they were undisciplined individuals who tired of inaction and indecisive results quickly.

If his war party abandoned the battle, the soldiers would leave across the plains. They would return again and again with more and more force until the Cheyenne and their buffalo, and their brothers, the Sioux and the Arapaho, would all be dead and the white man would take over this land.

"No, we must stop them now," thought Whirlwind Horse, "they are soldiers and their people know they are here. If they are wiped out by the Cheyenne in a mighty battle, maybe the White Grandfather will hear of it and put out his hand to stop this senseless rejection of their own treaty. They had been so anxious for all the tribes to sign treaties. Here, they are few and we are many. This is our chance to save the people and their buffalo.

All through the night, Whirlwind Horse did not sleep but tried to make a plan for the third day. That night, many other Cheyenne were also thinking about their lost friends and wanting revenge, or waiting to break off the fight and leave. These also did not sleep and darkness soon faded into dawn.

NINE

Inside their fortification, the U.S. troops also spent the night without much sleep. They woke intermittently expecting a night attack. Every few hours, the indians on the mountain above the soldier camp would fire wildly into the enclosure from the safety of the trees and under cover of darkness. The first time, the jittery soldiers returned the fire but Captain O'Meara then ordered no return shots unless they could see a target to shoot at. Neither side scored a hit and, after midnight, the indians fired no more volleys. This lack of activity, however, spread fear of an all-out night attack among the defenders and no one got much rest.

At first light of dawn, Captain O'Meara and Jim Early made the rounds of their defense perimeter checking on the troops and encouraging them to be alert and ready for anything. No shots were fired at them during this time as they moved around the enclosure.

Everyone had rations, water and ammunition. Satisfied all the men were awake and that their force was properly distributed, Early and O'Meara paused by a wagon in the center of camp to talk about their predicament. Lt. Turnock joined them.

"Jim, if we get out of this alive, how do we move the troop, without our horses, to Fort Lincoln?" O'Meara asked.

"We walk." Jim answered. "We'll have to cover several hundred miles on foot and cavalry boots will make mincemeat of our feet. You better give orders for everyone to put on any other boots or footwear they may have. I have a pair of heavy bullhide moccasins that I got from a squaw at Fort Yankton - these." He pointed to his feet.

"I know that Lt. Johnson has a pair of walking boots in his

gear. As small as he was, about the only one his boots would fit is Josiah. Josiah probably doesn't have any extra boots because he always rides on the cook's wagon on the trail." Lt. Turnock left to give Lt. Johnson's boots to Josiah and to pass the word to the rest of the troops. Most were already wearing their comfortable footwear anyway.

"Good point about the boots," O'Meara shot back testily, "but I was really wondering about what you think about our route to Lincoln. I'm hoping the indians will give up on riding over our rifles and go away. They don't usually like to engage in prolonged battle. I think their camp will break up soon if we hold here. Then, how do we get to Lincoln?"

"Northeast to the river, Captain," Jim answered. "Then follow along the river valley north until we get there. Because of the hostiles, we'll have to travel at night and hole up days. It will take us maybe three or four weeks. I think the terrain will be about like we saw coming west from Yankton across the Dakota prairie."

"On this end, there'll be good cover - deep brushy ravines will help us get away from the Black Hills. We'll only be able to bring what we can carry."

"That's what I figured. I'll start the preparations as we can..." O'Meara was distracted by thick, pungent smoke blowing into camp from the northwest on a stiff wind that had just come up since the calm of dawn. The sound of the prairie fire bearing down on them and gaining momentum every second was suddenly horrible and frightening.

"Damn it, Captain, the Cheyenne are trying to burn us out. That long grass is so dry it burns like kerosene this time of year!" Early shouted.

Soldiers all around started coughing from the acrid smoke. A forty-foot high wall of fire and heavy smoke blazed into the camp, followed by Whirlwind Horse's dog soldiers. The troops couldn't see to shoot until the screaming Cheyenne were on top of them. The brave men stood their ground firing with some effect until they were cut down, many with indian war axes, where they stood.

"Pull back!" O'Meara tried to rally his men and regain control. "Pull back". Just then, Lt. Turnock was shot full in the face by a point blank rifle shot. Sgt. Mueller killed two dog soldiers, as they closed on him, levering off two fast shots. As the soldiers backed away, firing, they formed a skirmish line across the enclosure, with a few troopers firing from under the wagons.

The fire and smoke slowed and as visibility improved, the firing from the troops caused the Cheyenne heavy casualties. Riderless horses bolted around the fortification and through the troops causing more confusion and problems for the army company. Hoop rode through the center of camp, torching the army wagons, forcing troops out from under those shelters and into the general fray. Early shot Hoop dead off his horse. The battle-hardened scout and Sgt. Mueller made every shot count with their repeaters against the front line of the advancing indians.

There were too many Cheyenne in their midst. As the troops fell back to the east edge, Captain O'Meara was using his pistols, with great effect, until suddenly, he fell over Grant knocking Grant down and pinning him down under the Captain. As Grant struggled to get free, he realized O'Meara was dead as he saw an arrow had penetrated deep into the center of the Captain's forehead. Horrified, Grant rolled down the ravine on the east end, apparently undetected. Gasping for breath, he took a position behind a boulder with his rifle ready.

A Cheyenne came running down the ravine with his battle axe raised. Grant pulled the trigger but the firing pin clicked on an empty chamber. The indian closed for the kill but a shot rang out from behind a nearby boulder. Josiah's true aim and single-shot Springfield saved the life of the son of the President of the United States of America.

Grant was glad to be alive but not grateful. The indian's bloody face stared lifelessly in Grant's direction. With a small shudder, Grant looked away and paid no more attention to either the dead man or his savior.

In a volley of shots, both Mueller and Early came over the top of the ravine and ran down the rough slope as fast as they could run. They were joined by Grant and Josiah in the boulders at the bottom of the mountain. In the confusion of fire and smoke, riderless horses, and with dead soldiers and dead indians all around, they had escaped without being noticed.

Among the Cheyenne, believing all the troopers dead, there was a general feeling of celebration now in the former army fortification. They were not looking for survivors.

During the attack, the main front of the grass fire diverted to the north side of the promontory and raged through the tall grasses there. After the battle, the fire was dying out as it ran out of fuel everywhere. Pungent smoke filled the air but the excited braves paid little attention to that distraction. Eyes watered, and coughing could be heard amid the din of exuberant yells of hundreds of Cheyenne celebrating their victory.

Braves raced for scalps and some angry confrontations erupted when two or more arrived at a trooper's body at the same time intending to count coup and lift the hair. Many warriors raced around on their ponies firing arrows or bullets into the dead bodies, yipping and yelling. Frightened, stray ponies reared and ran around the enclosure.

Spotted Horse found the bodies of Murphy and Atwood under blankets where they had been placed. The detached scalps were with their bodies. After lifting a couple scalps from other bodies from the early fighting, Spotted Horse found Tall Bear and gave him the two teamster's scalps. Atwood's and Murphy's trophies properly belonged to him.

The entire indian camp, including Owl Woman and the other women, had come in from the mountain top. Everywhere, the people were stripping all the clothing off the dead troopers, leaving their naked mounds of bloodied white flesh where they had fallen in battle.

Whirlwind Horse sat on his white pony off to the side and watched the desecration and carnival of hate unfolding before him. No one could hate the whites more than he. He did not, however, have the stomach for this senseless butchery of the fallen enemy who had fought bravely and well to the death in the face of overpowering odds.

There was no point in trying to interfere. The dog soldiers had earned all the spoils of war by wiping out the yellowleg troop and

Whirlwind Horse knew the hated whites had often done as much to the Cheyenne - even to women and children. They had cut off men's private parts to tan for tobacco pouches and women's to decorate their campaign hats. The whites had scalped and mutilated dead families in massacres in the villages, right where they fell at their very lodges. The madness here would go on for hours.

Whirlwind Horse slowly rode around the cavalry camp. He noticed that the body of Captain O'Meara had not been scalped. The war chief dismounted, held tightly to his pony's lead rope, and bent down to look at the cavalry leader's hair. Whirlwind Horse could immediately see why the Captain had not been scalped. O'Meara's thick, black hair had thinned at the crown of his head forming a circle of baldness at the part of the scalp most prized by the indians.

Since the taking of a scalp transferred the power of the enemy to the new owner, no one wanted it because the circle was bare where the power lives. Whirlwind Horse dropped O'Meara's head. The shaft of the Cheyenne arrow again pointed skyward from the Captain's forehead.

Whirlwind mounted his pony and rode off to check on the U.S. branded horse herd that Grey Blanket had stolen from the troop. The white war pony plodded up the mountainside and over the top to the west. The slow ride felt good, being alone and letting the warm, clean air blow away the bad thoughts and feelings.

Had he gone down the way Grey Blanket had gone and around the promontory, he might have found the survivors hidden in the rocks at the bottom of the mountain, but the Cheyenne didn't realize any white had survived the attack. Whirlwind Horse casually rode toward, and then past, the mountaintop indian camp and into the high valley where the horse herd grazed. The cavalry mounts tossed their heads in alarm when the chief appeared out of the timber but gradually settled down when he pulled his pony up and sat watching the herd.

TEN

IN THE ROCKS, LOOKING out across the prairie, Jim Early was assessing the predicament the four now found themselves in. "We'll have to move at night. We can't cross this open flat in daylight from here to where we can get cover in that ravine. They're busy up there, but there are several hundred of them, and someone would see the movement."

"We'll probably have to travel at night all the way to Lincoln. Without horses, it'll be hard going. We'll stick to the creek bottoms until we get to the river. We'll have the most cover, we can drink water anytime, and we can usually find shade in the daytime. We can probably find berries and small animals but we usually can't have cooking fires. It'll probably take us a month to cross all the way to Fort Lincoln."

Early was interrupted by a low moan. "Josiah, you're bleeding. Let's see that arm." Josiah grimaced with pain as Early peeled back the bloody shirt. Blood oozed from a large bullet hole. Jim gently pressed the surrounding area with his fingers to assess damage, touching the back of Josiah's arm with his right hand. Josiah winced. The bullet had gone through without hitting bone and left the same size hole in back. Josiah leaned back against a large rock in the shade. He closed his eyes to rest and gather strength.

Jim cut the tail off Josiah's shirt and fashioned cloth compress pads for both wounds. He wrapped a long piece of the cloth over the pads, around the arm, and tied it tight. "Should be all right until we get to Fort Lincoln, Josiah."

Privately, Early worried about infection and complications but he had done all he could with practically nothing to work with. Jim had seen men die in the war with trifling, non-threatening wounds simply because no treatment or clean bandages were available in the field. He secretly hoped this brave young black man could make it.

Technically, Jim thought, Fred Grant should be in charge here because of his temporary commission of Lt. Colonel USA. Just out of the "Point" and really only a Second Lieutenant, young Grant was not inclined to command but deferred to experience in situations where important decisions had to be made. He expected someone else to take care of him.

The President's son was along for the ride, preferring drinking and carousing. He intended to use his army position to further his own pleasures. Not much fun coming up in the next month or so, the scout mused. At the moment, Captain O'Meara's blood was dried all over the front and sleeve of Grant's shirt, but he was uninjured.

"Nasty looking head wound, Sgt." Jim turned to Mueller.

"Go to hell, Early. I still have my scalp. You take care of your nigger, I'll take care of myself." Mueller had dried blood caked in his hair and down the side of his face and onto his uniform shirt. He leaned his head back against the rock and closed his eyes. The hot August sun beat down without mercy. No breeze stirred to relieve the misery of the trapped men. Heat waves shimmered above the prairie to the east.

Jim checked to see if they had any guns left. He still had his short-barreled Colt with a handful of cartridges. Josiah and Grant had thrown away their empty rifles and both were unarmed. Sgt. Mueller had a service revolver stuck in his waistband but neither Mueller nor Early still had a rifle.

No one had water or food. The indians had it all in their former encampment above. "We're lucky to be alive", Early thought, as they waited out the long, hot summer afternoon.

His pistol on a rock close at hand, Jim noticed movement about fifty yards away on the prairie. It was Jube. He had broken away from the other horses as Grey Blanket escaped with the herd. He stood grazing, facing east, away from Jim and the others.

Jim hoped Jube wouldn't wander too far away before dark because it would be much easier to escape if the four survivors could take turns riding ... or if someone could ride who couldn't walk ... or if someone could ride ahead for help ...

The scout's calculations were cut short as indians shouted above and a torrent of Cheyenne shots cut down the horse. Jube fell, kicking, to the ground. There was a lot of shouting and laughing up there. Jube made pitiful moaning sounds for some time as he lay on the prairie. Jim was frustrated that he couldn't move to put his horse out of his misery. Finally, Jube's body quivered one last time and he lay quiet.

The Cheyenne nation was a job for the army, too big for one man to bring vengeance on. The indians had killed his companions and even his horse but they were protecting their own and had outgeneraled the troop in battle. Losing Jube reminded him again of Rose and his vow to avenge her death. Losing Rose was personal and the bear needed to be killed by Jim alone. He would always be tormented until he could come back for the bear. Rose's sweet memory and horrible death haunted Early.

The Cheyenne settled down to rest in any shade they could find. They had found the officers' whiskey cache in a wagon of stores. Empty whiskey cases were strung around the encampment and many of the dog soldiers had their own bottle. An occasional whoop rang out as testimony to their drunken condition but it was generally quiet as the indians succumbed to exhaustion, heat, and whiskey. Most passed out among the dead on the bloody battlefield. Whirlwind Horse rejoined his camp, riding in and turning his white pony loose.

ELEVEN

Darkness finally came, after the army men had suffered through the hot afternoon that seemed to them like it would never end. This was another dark night due to the cloudy, overcast sky. Jim thought that timing of their movements needed to be carefully planned with an eye to the sky because, occasionally, the clouds would part and moonlight would flood the countryside.

One at a time, they crossed the open space undetected and slipped into the ravine, safe now from observation by the enemy who were finally behind them. Early was bathed in sweat, the night was still hot. He worried about being quiet enough as they moved with agonizing slowness away from the Cheyenne. The strain of escaping took its toll on the scout. He felt heavy responsibility to see that he and his companions arrived safely at Fort Lincoln.

All the others were miserable too. Mueller and Josiah had a lot of pain from their wounds as they started moving. Grant's upper face and forehead and his forearms were badly sunburned because he had fallen asleep and had not moved with the shade for an hour or so during the afternoon in the rocks.

All of them had seen so much destruction and death and had lived in fear of being found for so many hours that they were all acutely conscious of the need to move quietly away from the danger behind them. Jim led them carefully, according to his plan, northeasterly away from the Hills and toward safety.

Mueller was thinking about killing Early before they would get to Lincoln. His head pulsed with pain and his thoughts were consistent with the time of war not so long ago when the enemy was from the south and killing the enemy was the main priority. To Mueller, the scout was a reb and worthless.

Grant was half-crazed with fear and horror remembering the attack and Captain O'Meara's death. When he was a boy he had been in his father's command tent when the elder Grant commanded the Union Army in the war between the states but Fred had not seen anyone die that he knew. His father had sheltered him from that. At West Point, everything had seemed a game. Now, the deaths of close acquaintances, especially with O'Meara at his side, and the destruction of the troop that had seemed so invincible, was hard for Grant to bear.

Josiah had survived slavery as a boy, escape from slavery, battles in the war and now brutal Indian attack, but his heart was pounding like a war drum and he thought surely the Cheyenne would hear the sound. No one spoke, even in whispers, and everyone moved carefully, avoiding making any slight noise.

At dawn, the four survivors were ten miles away from the Cheyenne. They had stayed in the bottoms, all dry land but easy going. Jim always turned north or east when any ravine they were following came to a dead end and a choice of new direction became necessary. All were exhausted. Early had kept them moving all night without rest or food or water in order to be a safe distance from the war party by daylight. For some time they had not been moving as carefully as they had moved at first. Jim felt that getting as far away as possible was more important.

Before the waning night was gone, Early climbed the dusty, brushy north bank of the ravine at the highest point to survey the country around them and saw they were only about a mile south of a river valley. He ran and slid back down to his companions to talk them into one last big effort before they hid out for the day.

"We're about a mile from what I believe is the Cheyenne River. According to a rough map I saw at the military briefing they gave me in St. Louis, we should be able to follow that river all the way to the Missouri. It runs generally northeast to the Missouri which will put us close to where we're heading when we hit the big river."

"To hell with you, Early, if you think I'm climbing up that mud hill right now," Mueller said.

"Stay here then. The rest of us want to get to water and there's a lot more cover where we can hide from wandering hostiles and stay out of the sun while we lay over days. We have to go right now before it's light so we can't be seen moving across. It's wide open from here to this river."

Without a word, Grant and Josiah got up and followed the scout as he started up the hill again. When they were half way up the hill, Mueller reluctantly followed. Like them, his mouth and throat were parched, and he didn't much like being alone and maybe losing contact with the others. His body quivered from exhaustion and his head throbbed unmercifully, but he forced himself to follow. Years of military hardship and discipline stood Mueller in good stead as he slowly moved up the steep bank, sometimes staggering and stumbling but always moving forward.

When they reached the river, Jim found a washed out hole in the opposite river bank, big enough for them to hide in. Jim checked it out while the others drank their fill of river water. His companions entered the small cave that widened out inside the opening.

Jim took a drink and looked around. Sure that they were unobserved, he washed the burning alkali prairie dust from his face and arms as the others had already done. He gathered a few pieces of driftwood and stacked it carelessly in front of the opening as camouflage. Then, he backed into the cave to collapse and sleep in cramped positions with the others.

TWELVE

IN THE PRE-DAWN DARK the morning after the battle, Cheyenne were moving all over the former cavalry fortification. Still jubilant, they shouted repeatedly to each other "we killed them all."

They sang kill-songs made up on the spot. Everyone was proud of having defeated the hated army. Much credit went to Whirlwind Horse for his leadership. Deeds of valor by Grey Blanket, Hoop, Tall Bear, and others were recounted many times.

As dawn brightened, family members and friends gathered up the bodies of their fallen Cheyenne comrades. After painting their dead faces with bright colors, wrapping them tightly in buffalo robes, and placing them on horse travois, they moved them to separate spots in the timber above the battle scene and laid them out on the ground.

Rocks were piled over the bodies to keep the coyotes from ravaging the remains. The indians ignored the bodies of the troops and the many ponies scattered around the battlefield. Crows and magpies were already landing and pecking at the eyes and raw areas on these bodies. Downwind, coyotes were picking up the scent. Twenty miles away, the huge grizzly that had killed Rose dropped to all fours and started toward the source of the smell of carrion.

Cheyenne women built roaring fires and boiled huge pots of buffalo stew in iron kettles from the army wagons. Most of the people had finished eating and were preparing to start north to their winter camp, when several young warriors drove up the U.S. horse herd.

Whirlwind walked through the herd and picked a sorrel, a big black, and a well-formed bay for himself. His headmen and certain warriors picked out individual animals to bring back as spoils of war. Some warriors had cavalry carbines now and ammunition for them from the ammo wagon. Headmen were the proud owners of the Spencers from the command, and all had clothing and souvenirs from the dead troopers.

Several horse travois were loaded with dried meat, coffee, and other foods from the supply wagons. Nothing of value to the indians was left behind. They systematically destroyed water barrels, the rest of the whiskey, and any part of the troops' wagons that were unburned.

At about mid-day, the Cheyenne party started north towards camp in the foothills of Paha Sapa. Many warriors carried scalp poles with trooper scalps swinging from the tips. Almost all wore army clothing which had been altered to suit the wearer. Breeches seats were often cut out, some tunic sleeves were ripped off and the coat worn open. A brass bugle hung over one brave's chest. Whirlwind Horse carried Captain O'Meara's field glass and Jim Early's field glass was a toy for Spotted Horse.

The indians talked animatedly for a long time with great pride about winning the battle and killing all the soldiers. A jubilant, festive feeling prevailed. As they rode out of sight, raising a towering cloud of dust from the hot prairie, vultures flew overhead and coyotes slunk into the abandoned battlefield.

THIRTEEN

ON A HIGH ROCKY ridge in the center of the Hills, the great male grizzly with the silver face was working his way toward the dead men and horses. Occasionally, he would rear up on his hind legs and test the wind for the scent he was following but most of the time he just headed into the wind and the ripe smell was unmistakable. By now, the bodies on the battlefield were bloated and stinking in the hot August sun.

The indian bodies added to the overall scent, too, since they were not buried in earth but just covered with rocks. Although, the rock piles would stop coyotes as the Cheyenne intended, piles of rocks would not prove difficult for the bear as a barrier between him and the bodies he could smell under them.

Hours after the Cheyenne departed, the big bear burst out of the trees above the battlefield running full speed, roaring and growling fiercely, straight into the former cavalry camp.

The silver faced bear charged a coyote standing nervously on a trooper body. The bear was very fast and the coyote hesitated, surprised and not willing to leave his newly found feast. With a swing of its mighty paw, the grizzly knocked the coyote through the air ten feet away and the coyote limped away yelping and whining.

Then, the bear turned and ran the length of the battlefield, feinting at the other coyotes who did not make the same mistake as the first one. They backed away nervously from this terrifying brute who had suddenly appeared and didn't seem to want to share with the other scavengers.

The big grizzly ran around and around among the dead bodies until he had the respect of the coyotes, the birds, and the vultures who all backed off. The bear stopped by a dead pony in the center of the enclosure, threatening the others with teeth gnashing, growls and roars.

The bear started to feed on the pony, keeping an eye on the other scavengers and occasionally growling or roaring at them. The others waited until the grizzly was concentrating on his meal and seemed to have forgotten them.

At first, the crows and magpies dropped down out of the trees at the southeast edge of the promontory. The bear watched but didn't even growl - just kept eating. The birds didn't immediately go to the bodies, but watched the bear and walked around. A vulture dropped in on a trooper body and began tearing flesh with his beak. Then a coyote tentatively returned to a body he had backed away from. Soon all the predators were eating again, but they left a wide space between themselves and the bear. The bear didn't look up. When the grizzly felt full, he walked away from the dead pony and lay down, still watching his own food supply.

Smaller predators came and went. The grizzly was at the time of year when he must store fat for his winter hibernation and he relished the rotting meat as much as the vultures did. He stayed at this gruesome banquet for two weeks before he started west across the hills to den.

Although it might be another month before he would actually enter his cave high in the limestone country of the western Hills, there was a cool nip in the night breezes now that foretold the time when his world would be buried in snow and ice for six months.

The giant bear had again eaten human flesh, again easily obtained without a fight or any danger. He would never forget the human smells and would forever identify them as a food source.

FOURTEEN

Seven sleeps after Whirlwind Horse's party left the scene of the great victory over the yellow-leg pony soldiers, they neared their home village late in the day. The party did not ride to their lodges and women, but stopped short and camped overnight to prepare for their return appearance. Whirlwind's party was close enough to the village to hear the dogs bark, but were camped over a rise in the prairie by a small stream, out of sight of the main camp.

Here, the men burned willow branches and painted their faces with the powdered charcoal mixed with water. Many painted their faces all black, the victory color for personal adornment. Some painted stripes or spots. Some of the men made drums. At dawn, they all dressed in the clothing they had worn in the battle.

Whirlwind Horse, carrying the pipe, mounted his white pony and led the procession. Warriors with scalps on poles were close behind, followed by Grey Blanket and Tall Bull, then a broad line of others who had shown courage in battle. Behind them rode the main body of returning warriors. The leaders charged into the teepee circles and along the lodges by the river at a gallop, firing their guns in the air to wake up the village and to announce their return. Those who followed beat their drums and fired their rifles as they advanced on the village.

The people poured out of their lodges to welcome the braves with excited yells. The women threw their arms around their men and sang songs of victory as they learned the news. Everyone admired the tall cavalry horses and the other spoils of war proudly displayed by the returning victors. Families of those who rode in the front rank would make gifts to friends or to poor people in honor of their own successful warrior.

Members of the war party went to their own lodges and turned out their horses. Their women and many of their children and relatives blackened their faces in preparation for dancing the scalp dance to celebrate the victory. Families of the warriors killed in battle realized their sons and husbands and fathers weren't returning and started keening in their lodges. Many had been killed by the pony soldiers - the Cheyenne had paid a high price. Loud wailing for the dead rose all over the village.

Moon Star mourned the death of Hoop. They had already made eyes at each other. He had courted her by playing the medicine flute one beautiful evening before he left on the hunting party that had turned into deadly war. Moon Star had planned to be Hoop's wife and to take care of him and his lodge. She stayed in the lodge of her father, Eagle-Who-Attacks, for three days before she emerged to again take up daily life. It would be a long time before the beautiful, sad maiden would again entertain advances from any would-be suitor.

Death in battle was considered to be glorious for any warrior so most of the grieving families of the dead braves slowly joined the scalp dance to honor the valiant ones. Kill-talks between the returning warriors and the families and excited young boys went on day and night during the scalp dance. Much honor was heaped on Whirlwind Horse, Grey Blanket, Tall Bull, Hoop, and the others who had come into camp in the front rank. No one slept much until the dance had run its course.

The people could hardly believe the Whirlwind and his dog soldiers had wiped out the pony soldiers war party. With their captured horses, guns and ammunition, the Cheyenne band was now much better prepared for any future engagements, if any were necessary. Most in the camp, however, believed that the blue soldiers would stay away from Paha Sapa now and the people could live in peace hunting their buffalo.

Surely, the wide eyes and their Grandfather far away would learn not to enter this land, which they had agreed by their own treaty would belong to those who had always lived here as long as the grass grows. Rejoicing ran through the village like a prairie fire, hot and wild.

Whirlwind Horse entered his lodge and sat on his blanket and leaned on his back rest at the rear of the teepee, facing the door opening. Having lost his family in the Sand Creek massacre of the southern Cheyennes, he had married again since he came north. His wife, Pretty Voice, had cooked buffalo hump meat and now gave him some in a bowl and a buffalo horn spoon to eat with.

Pretty Voice watched her husband as he ate. He was a famed leader, a strong man, a caring husband. She admired him and was glad she shared his robes. She was the envy of all the other women in the village.

As he finished eating, she knelt beside him and threw her arms around him and kissed him. With one smooth, quick move, Whirlwind Horse rolled her onto his sleeping robes and they were lovers before anything else got done that day.

In the middle of the afternoon, Whirlwind Horse and Pretty Voice left their lodge and walked to the victory dance. Whirlwind wore new clothes made by Pretty Voice while he had been gone. His shirt was soft smoke-tanned antelope skin decorated with colorful quill work and tufts of old scalps in two rows down the front.

The pants and moccasins were made of smoke-tanned horse hide. The tanning process gave the leathers a dark color. She had sewed a strip of red blanket down each leg of the pants and decorated the moccasins with more quill work.

Pretty Voice was one of the best quill workers in the village, as good as the old ones who had so many years of practice. The grandmothers had taught her well and she had quick hands and pride in her work.

Whirlwind Horse wore his hair in two braids, as was the custom in camp, with crow feathers intertwined. His face was painted with black victory paint and red war paint. Pretty Voice wore a new antelope-skin dress and moccasins tanned a light natural color and decorated also with fancy quill work.

The weather was beautiful. The sun was warm but not hot and a cool breeze came out of the west. It was the time of year when the leaves on the oak trees and the quaking aspen still wore the green of summer but would soon be turning to gold.

As he approached the dance, Whirlwind peeled off his shirt and pants, down to a breech clout, and handed them to his wife. He immediately joined the dancing warriors. Whirlwind Horse was the largest man in his village. His well-muscled, dark- skinned body stood out in contrast to most of the other light-skinned Cheyennes. He was a commanding figure, a natural leader.

Pretty Voice sat down on the trade blanket next to her younger sister, White Calf; her mother, Magpie; and her cousin, Owl Woman. Owl Woman, who had been with the dog soldiers at the battle, had many tales to tell and passed on the kill-talk of the warriors she had heard on the way back to the lodges. There were occasional gales of laughter from the happy women as their bodies swayed to the rhythm of the drum.

Six singers sat around the large drum and pounded out the beat with padded sticks. An old camp dog lay at their feet. Two young boys and two old men squatted in the dust close to the singers. The singers constantly sang shrill songs of battle and of victory.

The celebration swelled as most of the big village joined the gala festivity. As the sun descended toward the western horizon, the singers stopped and young boys brought them dippers of cold river water. The dippers were fashioned from buffalo gut suspended from the ends of long forked sticks.

After new singers took their places at the drum, the women danced in honor of their dead and sang of the bravery and success of the war party. Young girls, little girls, even very old women joined in. They were all dressed in their best clothing with colorful feathers and fancy quill work decorations. There were old songs everyone knew, and new songs telling how the hated whites had fallen down before these brave men and had given them their big horses and fast-talking guns.

Whirlwind Horse sat on Pretty Voice's blanket now vacated by the dancing women. Some other warriors sank down to rest with him. Small boys ran through the crowd pretending battle and generally being in the way of the revelers but no one cared.

Dipper boys brought fresh water to the seated men - first to the war chief, then to the others. Flies buzzed around and the men picked up the bird wing fans and buffalo tails, left by the women, to ward off and to swat the unending pests.

The men settled in to tell the often repeated kill stories and honor stories about the battle. Young boys gathered to listen to the verbal history that they in turn would pass on to generations yet to come. This was the way the Cheyenne knew of and were inspired by old stories of their grandfathers and even of their grandfathers' grandfathers still told by the old ones in the village.

At sunset, the western sky was red and purple fading out to pink along the horizon. Scattered clouds across the sky and over Paha Sapa were a delicate shell pink. The shadows deepened and the firelight flickered over the women who still danced. Whirlwind Horse looked fondly at Pretty Voice as she danced in his honor but he also looked with interest upon White Calf, his sister-in-law.

White Calf had many suitors among the young braves but she had never given favorable sign to any. She was a happy, laughing, high-spirited young woman - not as shy and soft spoken as Pretty Voice. There had been three winter counts since Whirlwind Horse and Pretty Voice had been married but still they had no children.

Cheyenne custom directed that war chiefs and village chiefs should have at least two wives but not more than four. Multiple wives among the Cheyenne were often sisters which usually contributed to more harmony in the lodge than if the wives came from different families.

When a Cheyenne man wanted to marry his wife's sister, if their parents found his presents suitable, he had preference over any other suitor and usually took the sister for another wife. If, however, the sister wanted to marry a different suitor instead, the brave she wanted had to make presents to her sister's husband as well as her parents in order to take precedence and win the wife.

Whirlwind Horse was thinking it might be time to take his second wife. Just then his eyes met the eyes of the dancing White Calf as she flashed a glance in his direction. She let her glance linger momentarily and then danced away.

White Calf knew all about the ancient marriage customs of the tribe and she wanted to marry this man more than she valued life itself. His impressive appearance in the dance with the other warriors was not lost on her. She had watched him longingly but secretly during the afternoon. No one had noticed. She had felt this way for a long time. She allowed others to come to her as suitors but she wanted no other but Whirlwind Horse.

In the dark of the second night of the scalp dance, after dancing furiously, Whirlwind Horse felt chilled as he sat alone at the edge of the dance. Pretty Voice was with friends in the shadows on the other side beyond the fire and the dancers.

The Whirlwind got up and went to his lodge for a warm robe to wrap around himself. The soft skin felt good against his tired body. As he was heading for the blanket to sit down again, he noticed the rest of the dancers were tired and leaving the dance. The singers had stopped singing but they still beat the drum. The savage rhythm pounded in his temples.

Whirlwind saw that White Calf was standing directly ahead of him in the shadows at the edge of the firelight looking away from him towards the fire. He walked up behind her, and holding his robe open with both hands, his arms outstretched, he put his arms around White Calf, folding both of them inside his robe. They stood together as young lovers might stand.

White Calf's heart pounded. She didn't have to look to know the powerful body embracing her was Whirlwind Horse. She knew this meant he was claiming her and he would ask for her in marriage. She was very happy.

They talked quietly about trivial things, in the Cheyenne way at such times, but not about love or each other. Unspoken, that was in their feelings for each other. They stood talking in this way until the fire died down and many people saw them and talked of it.

Pretty Voice went to their lodge and lay down in their sleeping robes as though she were asleep. Later, Whirlwind Horse entered the lodge quietly and prepared for bed. As he slid under the skins, his arm brushed Pretty Voice's bare back but she did not move and he was soon asleep. Tears fell from Pretty Voice's eyes. She woke often through the night and was up at daybreak.

FIFTEEN

When Whirlwind Horse woke up, the sun was hitting the tops of the teepee poles. Pretty Voice had made coffee from the supply taken from the army stores. Together, they ate strips of dried buffalo meat and drank hot coffee without much talk between them. After eating, Whirlwind went for a swim in the cold river below the camp, away from the eyes of the village. He swam long and the sun was warm when he climbed from the water.

He picked up a lead rope from his lodge and went to the horse herd. He couldn't catch his frisky paint pony, so he slipped a loop around his white pony's nose, mounted, and cut out the three U.S. branded horses he had claimed. The war chief also picked out a matched pair of black ponies which were favorites of his for riding. He drove the five horses to the lodge of White Calf's father, Grey Wolf, and turned them out behind the teepee where two of Grey Wolf's mustangs stood.

Whirlwind's mother-in-law, Magpie, was scraping a hide staked out on the ground nearby. These two did not speak because it was forbidden for the family matriarch and the normally independent young warrior husband to talk to each other.

Whirlwind found White Calf's brother, Young Wolf, and asked him to present the captured horses to Grey Wolf and to ask his father for White Calf to be Whirlwind's second wife. This was the Cheyenne way.

He knew he was giving Grey Wolf great honor by offering him the horses captured in battle. They were beautiful animals, well trained and capable of hauling much larger loads on travois than Indian ponies could. Young Wolf could keep the black ponies and Whirlwind also gave him a captured Springfield rifle and an ammunition belt full of shiny cartridges. Young Wolf smiled and turned to enter Grey Wolf's lodge. Magpie followed him inside to be in on the discussion.

In late afternoon, Young Wolf entered Whirlwind Horse's lodge to tell him that Grey Wolf and the family accepted his offer for White Calf in marriage. They sent presents of clothing, baskets, a new back rest for Whirlwind, and fresh deer meat taken that morning by Grey Wolf above camp.

As soon as Young Wolf left the lodge, Pretty Voice picked up a skin water bag and went up the river by herself. She was very unhappy and sad. Instead of being glad her own sister would be her husband's lawful second wife, Pretty Voice felt she was losing him to another woman.

When she was across the stream and out of sight of the village, she entered a deep draw and wailed as though her husband had died and she was in mourning. She threw herself down on the rocky ground and cried with deep sobs. Her grief consumed her. Eventually, she got up with a dull look in her reddened eyes, washed her face in the river and went back to the lodge.

Very little conversation passed between Pretty Voice and her husband while she prepared food and they ate. Whirlwind Horse understood the bad feelings of his wife because their marriage had been unmarked by any conflict and they had been very loving and close. He prayed by smoking the pipe silently and wished that she would be sensible and accept her sister into their lodge. He felt sure Pretty Voice would be whole again after a few sleeps.

They made love wildly that night. Afterwards, Pretty Voice held him in her arms and cried until she went to sleep. Whirlwind gently laid her over and went to sleep troubled.

As days went by and the wedding time of the next full moon approached, Pretty Voice was usually her old self but was sometimes quiet and withdrawn. She worked hard on new clothing for her sister which she decorated with her beautiful quill work.

Whirlwind Horse prayed with the pipe every evening. He felt that the healing was working on Pretty Voice and she would be ready to take her sister into the lodge when the time came. They would be a happy family together. Pretty Voice cleaned constantly inside and outside the lodge.

On the day of the marriage, White Calf sat on a buffalo hide at her father's lodge and Young Wolf and three of his friends picked up the skin at the corners and carried the bride to Whirlwind's lodge and across the threshold, setting her down gently in her new home. Then the young men left the lodge and went away.

White Calf had arrived wearing new clothing she and her mother had made. As she sat waiting, Pretty Voice entered, spoke to her sister and extended her hand to help her stand. Then, hand in hand they walked to the rear of the teepee and Pretty Voice undressed the second wife down to her virgin's chastity string.

The string was a soft rope of braided deer skin worn around the waist and between the legs with provision to lengthen as she had grown from girl to married woman. White Calf had worn hers for five winter counts.

In the Cheyenne tradition, Pretty Voice dressed White Calf in the new clothes she had made for her. Pretty Voice thought how beautiful her sister looked, flushed as she was with excitement and with some embarrassment that she was actually entering this lodge to share her sister's husband. When White Calf was fully dressed, Pretty Voice left the lodge and went with Magpie to Grey Wolf's lodge.

Only now did Whirlwind Horse enter his lodge and claim his new second wife. Custom allowed the new bride to continue wearing her string for about ten sleeps before the husband could take it off, but no longer. White Calf asked that this be done. So, the first night and the second night they lay together in the sleeping robes with only the string between them. They did not sleep but talked all night and slept off and on the following days.

On the third night, neither Whirlwind Horse nor White Calf could wait longer and the virgin's string was cast aside. A night of great passion followed. Exhausted, they were both still asleep when Pretty Voice entered with boiled deer meat after the sun was already warming the teepee. Whirlwind sat up and accepted the food and told Pretty Voice she should move back into their lodge after three more sleeps. Pretty Voice nodded. Turning to leave, she saw her sister's string where Whirlwind Horse had thrown it, near the entrance flap. Pretty Voice impulsively picked up the string and held it against her dress as she walked away. Tears stung her eyes again as she thought of her husband and her sister together.

Pretty Voice sat by Grey Wolf's lodge, fleshing a staked out deer skin with her mother's bone scraper. She stopped her work and picked up the string from the ground at her feet. She untied the ends of the braided rope, unfastened the piece that goes between the legs, then tied a hard knot to join the two pieces together into a straight rope as long as a boy is tall.

She formed a loop in one end like a nose loop in a pony lead before wandering away from the village carrying the rope. She found the place where she'd crossed the creek before on big rocks and through shallows, and made her way to the draw where she'd wailed her grief.

Idly, the confused and suffering woman played with the rope she now found in her hands. She passed the loose end around a sturdy tree at about chest level and through the loop. Holding the loose end, she lunged against the rope venting her pain and anger. The rope held and the knot tightened. She removed the rope from the tree trunk and slowly walked up the pine slope along the rim of the rocky ravine, stopping at a cliff-like spot above where she had been before. A small pine grew at the very edge of the caved off rim of the ravine.

Sitting on the forest floor of pine needles next to the tree, Pretty Voice tied the straight end of her rope around the tree trunk at the ground, dropped the loop around her neck, took a deep breath and rolled off the edge causing a sharp jerk when the weight of her body hit the end of the rope.

Pretty Voice uttered a small cry as she rolled off the edge which caused Young Wolf to look towards her as he was passing the mouth of the ravine. He was returning from a deer hunt in the Hills with two deer loaded on his pony travois.

The jerk on the hanging rope snapped the shallow roots of the young tree. Pretty Voice tumbled down the slope to the bottom, pulling the tree behind her. The loop had tightened around her neck so that she couldn't possibly breathe. She lay still with her head at an odd angle.

Young Wolf ran to her side and pulled the loop loose which required all of his strength. It seemed the leather had grown together against Pretty Voice's neck. She lay still as he removed the rope from her neck. She had an ugly, raw, deep scrape on her neck and wasn't breathing. Her eyes were closed and her head faced sideways.

Young Wolf picked her up with his hands under her arms and dragged her body to his horse. He quickly untied and unloaded the deer. When he turned to pick Pretty Voice up, she moved and sighed. He lashed her to the travois and kicked his pony to its best speed back to the village.

Whirlwind carried Pretty Voice into their lodge and gently placed her on the sleeping robes. After Young Wolf told what happened, he went to tell Grey Wolf and Magpie. Whirlwind and White Calf took care of this beautiful woman who tried to take her life because of them. She did not wake up until after dark but she was breathing regularly and sometimes moved her head from side to side. Whirlwind Horse prayed with the pipe while White Calf rubbed her sister's face and arms and kept cool, wet skins on her forehead.

Grey Wolf brought the old medicine man, White Bull, to Whirlwind's lodge. After a quick look, White Bull prayed to the bear for her strength to return and to the antelope for her grace and quickness. By the time Pretty Voice woke up, White Bull was outside wailing his eerie chant to the sky. Neighbors gathered nearby, talking softly among themselves.

When Pretty Voice opened her eyes, she was looking into White Calf's anxious, concerned face and she instinctively clutched White Calf's hand in her hands in a show of love for her sister. Pretty Voice's resentment and anger were now gone and she was ready to live with Whirlwind Horse and a second wife, her sister, together in harmony.

She felt foolish for her earlier feelings and for trying to take her own life. She also now was very afraid of death and, for the rest of her life, she would sometimes wake up screaming in the night after she imagined the feeling of the noose tightening around her neck.

Pretty Voice gradually gained strength, could talk again and resumed her wifely duties and privileges. By the time the snow settled on their camp in the moon of the popping trees, Whirlwind and his wives were a happy family and love lived in their lodge.

SIXTEEN

THE MEADOWLARK SONG SOUNDED again at the edge of a mountain meadow near the north edge of Paha Sapa. The young Cheyenne, Red Fox, knew the signal was made by his friend. Red Fox kicked his pony's ribs with a bare heel and rode across the meadow to meet Sparrow Hawk.

Having tired of the battle against the bluecoat soldiers, and sure it would end with indian withdrawal, these two youths had melted into the trees together at daybreak on the third day of siege. They were soon over a ridge and into a valley west of the battlefield when the decisive battle took place. The boys heard nothing and went on their way, happy to be alone in this beautiful place to hunt and sleep under the stars.

Red Fox and Sparrow Hawk had been the best of friends all their lives. Had they known there would be another battle, they would have been excited to fight and would have stayed with the war party. There had been so much talk the second day about giving up the fight and just taking the big army horses back to the village, the pair grew tired of no action and went off by themselves to enjoy the late summer weather.

When the day grew hot, they could relax in the cool shade of the pines, or ride their ponies in the sun and talk about the battle of the first day. They ate some dried buffalo strips from the war camp and roasted rabbits and woodchucks over campfire coals. Berries and cold mountain spring water rounded out their sumptuous daily fare. At night, they slept comfortably on thick pine needle beds.

The young Cheyenne had been out about fifteen sleeps since they rode away from the war party. Nights were getting cold now and frost was on the grass in the mornings. They decided to hunt deer so they could take fresh meat back to the village. If they were successful today, they could ride on into camp in a couple days because their movement had been across the hills in the direction of the village. They were close to the swift river that flowed out on the plain where they knew the winter camp was located.

The friends laughed and talked in the meadow as their ponies champed the wild grasses nearby. The sun was high now and they would wait a few hours before riding out in separate directions again to look for deer. Neither had seen anything close enough to shoot with bow and arrow since daybreak today.

In late afternoon, Sparrow Hawk rode off up the hill south of the meadow in a westerly direction. Red Fox delayed until his friend was out of sight in the denser timber halfway up the sidehill and then rode west slowly along the edge of the meadow.

Sparrow Hawk stopped his pony and turned toward Red Fox below. He could see a deer crossing the meadow in a slight defile just ahead of Red Fox and heading in Sparrow Hawk's general direction. Sparrow Hawk dismounted and got ready with his bow and arrow. Near the bottom of the hill, the four-point whitetail buck crested out of the defile and stopped. Red Fox on horseback reached for his bow but the movement spooked the buck. The deer crashed noisily up the hill through brush, kicking loose clumps of dirt and rocks in his scramble towards Sparrow Hawk.

The buck passed a few yards above Sparrow Hawk and fell in mid-stride as the arrow struck deep behind his front leg piercing his heart. As the deer went down, he rolled to Sparrow Hawk's feet and bleated a dying cry. Hearing the young hunter's loud, exultant whoop, Red Fox started up the hill to help his friend with the kill.

After gutting out the fat buck, Sparrow Hawk dragged the deer down to the meadow as Red Fox rode ahead leading the Hawk's pony. At the meadow again, the young men hung up the buck to drain and cool, tying his antlers to a tree branch with Red Fox's pony lead rope.

The sun was setting and the young hunters squatted by a small fire talking about their luck. They planned to head for camp the next morning. They could reach the river tomorrow and the village the following day.

Suddenly, two thousand pounds of live, charging grizzly appeared out of the brush southeast of their small camp. The silver-faced bear raked the haunch of Red Fox's pony. The pony reared, screamed in terror, and ran away to the west, blood spurting from the deep claw marks. The bear attacked Sparrow Hawk's pony and killed it with a swipe of his paw as he advanced toward the hunters.

Red Fox froze momentarily in fear as Sparrow Hawk ran to a nearby tree. Red Fox's hesitation was his undoing as the grizzly overwhelmed him, took his head in his huge jaws and broke Red Fox's neck with one shake of his head. The bear's teeth sank into Red Fox's throat as he dragged the body along to the base of the tree which Sparrow Hawk was clambering up as high and as fast as he could go.

Through the night, the horrified Sparrow Hawk was trapped up the tree while the great bear devoured his dead friend below. In the middle of the night, the grizzly covered Red Fox's remains with a kill mound and ambled into the brush to rest where he could guard his kill.

Just before dawn, after suffering for many hours in the cold in the tree top, Sparrow Hawk decided maybe the bear was gone and that he should try to get away. He had climbed down only a few branches when the big grizzly, roaring furiously, charged out of the brush, to the base of the tree that was the Hawk's refuge. Sparrow Hawk scampered back up and wailed loudly in desperation. The bear stood on his hind legs and swatted above his head. Once, when he hit the tree, Sparrow Hawk heard a cracking sound in the live tree trunk.

Roaring ferociously, the grizzly started to climb the tree. Sparrow Hawk broke off a dead branch to use as a club and as the bear lunged upward, the Cheyenne reached down and struck him a good blow on the tip of his nose. The surprised bear lost his grip and fell out of the tree.

Enraged, the huge animal immediately started back up the tree. As the bear climbed, Sparrow Hawk inched higher and pulled his feet up. The bear was looking up and flailing over his head with one paw. All of this movement and weight caused the cracked tree trunk to break off, hurling Sparrow Hawk and the tree top to the ground.

Sparrow Hawk landed on his feet, crouched as he had been in the tree, and he ran as fast as he could along the edge of the meadow in the direction taken by Red Fox's pony. The pony, crazed with fear, had run a long way and was nowhere in sight.

The bear climbed down clumsily but when his rear paws hit the ground he whirled and dropped to all fours to race after Sparrow Hawk. It was no contest. The bear could run faster than a horse and he soon caught up with and killed the helpless boy. Once again, the grizzly settled down for two weeks to a horrible feast before moving toward his den.

Red Fox's pony moved down the watershed arriving at the river when the grasses were brown and the leaves of the trees and bushes were yellow and falling to the ground. The pony limped badly now as infection in his hind leg caused constant pain. Grey Wolf, riding out to hunt deer up the canyon of the river, found him lying down unable to get up. Grey Wolf shot him to end his misery. Grey Wolf recognized the mark of the much-feared bear and figured it must be enormous judging by the spread of the claw furrows in the horse's haunch. He also thought it would be surprising if either of the young warriors who were still missing would return now.

Snow fell in the high country that night as Grey Wolf rode back into the village with a fat whitetail doe and the Cheyenne settled in for the cold, snowy moons to come. There was sorrow in the lodges of the families of Red Fox and Sparrow Hawk.

The grizzly was at a higher elevation as he headed for den than the deer because they were moving lower for winter. The bear pounced on small game and he found a dead coyote frozen in the snow. He ate everything he could forage as his body became sluggish and he readied for his winter sleep.

The cold wind blew snow in the bear's face and riffled his thick fur as he stood on the limestone rim looking over a deep canyon. The huge silver faced bear dropped down the canyon wall to den up in his usual cliff cave where he would not be bothered through the hard, frozen months ahead.

SEVENTEEN

IN THE CAVE BESIDE the Cheyenne River, Early slept uneasily for a few hours and then was awakened by groans from Sgt. Mueller. Mueller slept on in spite of his wounds. The cave was cool and damp and clear of flies. Jim went to the opening and looked around. He couldn't see much, just along the river nearby. It was oven hot outside. He watched the water for awhile, then turned his attention to his comrades.

Josiah winced in his sleep as he bumped his wounded arm. Grant slept soundly even with his sunburn. Mueller had cuts on his face and on the backs of his hands and forearms. He had lost a lot of blood from his head wound. His hair was matted with dried blood and some fresh blood showed, oozing out.

The Cheyenne who had jumped him must have been strong and a good fighter. Mueller had killed the indian by Frenchman's creek and then barely made it to the troop before the battle started. He had used up his reserves during the fight, killing more than his share of the attackers and managing to stay alive. Then, he was still able to make ten miles to this little cave. Mueller was sure as hell tough and army to the core. Right now, though, he did not look ready to move on.

Early slipped out of the cave and did a quick recon of the immediate area. Seeing nothing threatening, he cut a large piece of green bark from a live birch tree, fashioned a bowl from it and filled it with river water. Back in the cave, Jim unwrapped Josiah's arm and soaked his wound pads until they were softened. He removed them and washed the arm clean. He washed out the shirt-tail pads, wrung them out and rebandaged the arm with the cool, clean cloths.

71

The bullet holes were not sealed but still bled as Jim worked, the blood washing out the inner wound. Josiah had pain in the arm but he settled back more comfortably and closed his eyes when Jim was through cleaning him up. With more clean water, Jim moved over to Mueller.

The sergeant was more than asleep, he was unconscious. Jim carefully pulled Mueller's pistol from the front of his pants, thoughtfully twirled the cylinder, and laid it out of Mueller's reach. Mueller didn't move. Jim moved up beside him and washed his hair and cleaned around the gash in the scalp. The long cut was deep and bleeding. Jim thought it should have stitches to pull the scalp together. No chance for that here.

With his sharp knife, the scout trimmed hair away from the wound. He cut a piece from Mueller's shirt and made a dry pad, then placed it over the length of the cut and pressing with the fingers of both hands, pushed the cut together. The cloth soaked with blood and dried as Early held it in place.

The improvised bandage stuck all around the wound and held the flesh together. Jim carefully washed the hair clean and wiped the blood and water from Mueller's face. Mueller groaned. Early stuck Mueller's revolver back in his waistband and moved away.

Late in the day, the scout carefully moved through trees along the river to a place where trees spread up the hill, affording cover to a high point from which he could make a good survey of the area. An eagle soared above the prairie, hunting on high air currents. As Jim watched, the eagle dove to the ground and came back up with a squealing rabbit. His big wings flapped as he flew away to his nest.

The blue sky was cloudless except for thunderheads building up over the Black Hills. Heat waves trembled over the listless buffalo and antelope as far as Jim could see. Hot. Even in the shade of the tall rock jutting above the hilltop, beads of sweat glistened on the scout's face and his clothes stuck to his body. Not a breath of wind stirred.

Jim lay on the hilltop, moving just his eyes or cautiously moving his head as little as possible. After about an hour of watching the animals and looking for movement or dust in the air, he was satisfied there were no hostiles nearby. He could see no campfire smoke or smell it. He eased off the top and back into the trees. Breaking off a leafy branch, he rubbed out some tracks, checking his trail for any sign of his passing.

Early stopped at a thicket of wild plum bushes along the river. He washed out his buckskin shirt and hung it on a bush to dry while he cleaned up in the river. He felt his beard stubble and wished he had a razor. When his shirt was dry, he picked about a gallon of the wild plums, eating some as he picked but dropping most of them onto his clean shirt to take back to the cave. The plums tasted sweet, delicious. He cleaned all the fruit out of the bushes before he headed again toward the others, walking in the water at the edge of the river.

When Early got back to the cave at sundown, he called the others out to clean up in the river. Josiah and Grant came out of the cave but Mueller was still groggy and unwilling to move.

"We'll stay here at least another day, maybe longer," Early told them, "we all need the rest and it looks safe here. Eat some wild plums and fill up on water, then crawl back in the cave and sleep as much as you can."

"Early," Grant said, "we need to put some distance between us and those redskins and get to civilization as soon as we can."

"Mueller and Josiah aren't in any shape to go on tonight. I agree with you, but we'll make better time when we're all healthier. Besides, we'll be on reservation all the way to the Missouri River and it will be possible to run into hostiles anywhere. We need to be as wide awake as we can be for the benefit of all of us."

"Cut the nigger loose. The rest of us will be better off. He's only one generation out of the trees. Let him take care of himself - one less mouth to feed," Grant said.

"Let's not forget this is the man who saved your life, Grant. He won't slow us down any and he deserves the same as we get, whether we make it or not. Josiah's in the game as far as I'm concerned."

Josiah cast his eyes away and said nothing. Grant grabbed a big handful of ripe plums, spit out a couple seeds and went inside the cave with Mueller.

Early addressed Josiah. "Stay close to me. We're all in this together. You're a free man and a soldier working for the same government. We'll all make it out, I swear."

Josiah shot a grateful glance at Early and helped him brush out sign as they backed into the cave together. Early looked up at the rain clouds fast approaching their hideout. This would be a good night to be in the cave, safe and dry. Early put the rest of the plums in a pile by Mueller and placed the water bowl in the center between them all. Then he settled down between Josiah and the others to rest.

Wild rain poured outside and the torrent of the river grew louder. The strain of the last few days had its way, and Early slept. Heavy breathing was general all around the little cave.

Hours later, Josiah rose up from his sleeping space, hot with fever and confused. He quietly went to the cave entrance and walked out into the rainy night. Water cascaded down his face and soaked his body. Josiah turned east along the river, haltingly stayed on the bank a ways, then walked right into the water.

The swift current picked him up and carried him along until he struck a long tree trunk that had fallen down across the river. Half drowned and gasping for breath, the instinct to survive took over and Josiah made his way to the other side of the river along the downed tree. He pulled himself out and staggered downstream, away from the hideout, and into the badlands river breaks. At dawn he collapsed face down on top of a rocky ridge. The rain was letting up but it had obliterated his tracks.

Sometime after Josiah left the cave, Early stirred and realized Josiah was gone. He woke Grant. "Josiah's gone, Colonel. It's still storming like hell outside. I'm going looking for him."

"Suit yourself, Early. Don't abandon us and take off by yourselves or I'll have your head. You're still US Army."

"Colonel, I'll find him and bring him back if he's alive. Don't leave this cave tomorrow if I don't get back by daylight. He can't be far away unless he fell in the river and washed away. I'll be back here tomorrow night and all of us will be better off if we stick together."

"Let the nigger go, Early. This is perfect. He left us and we sure as hell don't need him."

Jim ignored Grant. "Try to get some plums and water into Mueller. Maybe a little food in his belly will start him coming around. We can't stay here much longer."

Early took a deep breath and plunged out into the stormy night. It was difficult to decide which way the orderly had gone. He had to get his face down very close to the ground to see in the dim light, making him muddy as well as wet. Jim searched upstream. Maybe it was hopeless.

Finding nothing, he returned to the cave opening. In a lightning flash, he saw that Grant was asleep again. Turning east, Jim saw a spot where Josiah had slipped and fell. He felt with his fingers the deep marks in the mud that the rain hadn't washed out yet. "Maybe I'm soon enough to be able to track him," Jim said to no one but the rain and the wind.

Jim noticed plain sign in a protected spot near the water where the boot tracks headed straight into the river. Despair gripped him. How could anyone survive that current, especially someone as weak as Josiah with his wound? Squatting to examine the track, Early looked downstream and thought he saw a downed tree spanning half the river from the other side. He hurried down the river bank until he was opposite the tree bobbing in the wild water.

Early walked a little way back up stream and dived as far out as he could and swam hard to cross the river. The rushing water roared in his ears and tried to pull him under. The strong river swept him away but he made enough progress sideways to catch the current that carried Josiah to the tree. When he hit the tree, Jim pulled himself along and got out on the opposite bank. He quickly found deep boot prints in the mud at the river's edge showing Josiah had gone downstream but was veering away from the water. He rested before he took up the trail again.

EIGHTEEN

WHEN THE SUN CAME up in the east, a small rogue party of Sioux warriors rode up out of the badlands heading for Paha Sapa. These six had left their village along the Missouri River craving freedom and adventure. They were tired of the careful life of those who licked the white's boots and who always hoped for a handout but never got much. In their village, bellies were empty and babies cried.

The old ones in their village thought they must make peace with the whites. They remembered being pushed westward from the country of many lakes by other stronger tribes when they were young. They had called the Missouri River country home for many years before the white man came. This time, they would stay and learn to live with the new people.

Crow Bear and Spotted Elk and the other four in this party had tired of arguing with the old ones. Their band had ponies now that would allow them to move out into the reservation where the buffalo were everywhere. No one should be hungry now.

So, when Spotted Elk rode in with a small party of Sioux from the west in the time of the new pony colts and the calves dropping, Crow Bear and his friends listened to his stories with great interest. Spotted Elk told of growing up near Paha Sapa where there was clear water, plenty of buffalo, and still no whites.

This country was far out in the indian lands where the white man said he would never go. Spotted Elk told stories about the Great Bear God in Paha Sapa and about the mountain of snakes in the badlands.

Spotted Elk spoke of the White Buffalo Calf Woman. The old ones of his band said she appeared in a vision in the time of their grandfathers to tell them they should always live in this good country as long as the rivers flow and the grass grows. She promised that great herds of buffalo and deer would sustain them forever.

In the moon when the green leaves appeared, these six young Sioux left the village on the big river and rode away to the west. Before they had gone one sleep, they came upon a white farmer and his family who had strayed away from the river and set up camp in a green valley by a cold water spring. The young Sioux rode up when the farmer was out away from his cabin breaking ground for planting.

The small band killed the farmer and his stock, then his hysterical wife and children. They killed the wife and little girl only after brutally playing with them and raping them. They burned the house with the bodies in it and the shed that was a barn. They tore up everything that had belonged to the settlers and rode on, feeling they had partly evened the score with the whites.

On the morning after the big rain, this small band of renegades came upon Josiah, as they were coming up out of the badlands. Josiah was unconscious, unarmed and wounded. Spotted Elk had never seen a black white man before. The river indians called him a buffalo soldier because of his color and his matted, curly hair. They had seen a few of these troopers with the yellow-leg soldiers and even one or two with big hats that the whites called cowboys. The Sioux dismounted and squatted, eating dried buffalo meat while they watched this strange soldier. For a long time, Josiah didn't move.

One by one, the six Sioux stood up, talking about what to do with their helpless captive. The warriors searched the area for tracks but found none. Josiah came to, rolled over and sat up, and was instantly and visibly afraid. The indians laughed. One of the braves pricked the skin on Josiah's neck with a lance point and he bled red. The Sioux were surprised. Josiah had recovered his composure and barely winced when touched with the lance. The indians admired his bravery.

Jim Early was coming up the side of the ridge and his sharp eyes caught movement and color. He carefully moved closer with his loaded Colt drawn, and concealed himself in brush. Josiah was on the ground, too low for Jim to see from the sidehill. He had the drop on the Sioux but he might not be able to kill them all before they got him and then they would kill Josiah too.

Josiah came into view when the indians bound his hands, talking to each other all the time in Sioux. Didn't seem like they would bother tying him up if they were going to run a lance through him on the spot. Early stayed patient.

On the ridge, Spotted Elk spoke again of the mountain of snakes. The mountain was nearby on their way to Paha Sapa. He had been there in the spring several times and seen huge dens of snakes all tangled up in big balls in holes in the rocks on the mountain. It was said that the snakes wintered in these dens and came out in the spring and left the mountain during the hot summer, returning to den again about this time of year.

Spotted Elk's idea was to take this black white soldier to the mountain of the snakes and stake him out near a den and let the snakes have him. They all laughed, mounted up and led Josiah away to the west. Jim stayed in the brush and followed at a safe distance.

The sun was high when the indian band neared a large hole at the top of the snake mountain. Snakes coiled around the edge of the hole in the hot sun. Josiah was covered with sweat from fear and heat.

Many rattlesnakes crawled or lay coiled with their forked black tongues flicking in and out of their closed mouths. The indians had led Josiah around the snakes on their trip up the peak. From horseback they could spot the snakes soon enough to avoid them.

The Sioux spread-eagled Josiah in a wide, clear spot where snake trails converged near a den. Early worked in close, also being careful of the snakes. Nearby a huge rattler crawled, stretched out so he couldn't strike, his mouth opened wide, fangs dripping venom. That snake crawled away to hide in the grass and weeds.

Now, he was very jumpy, having seen more rattlers here than he ever imagined existed in the entire country. He was scared for Josiah. Maybe he should try to take the Sioux party. Something held him back but he didn't want to wait too long.

He wouldn't have much time - there were so damned many snakes. Jim was close, he could see the indians plainly. Again, Josiah was on the ground out of his sight. The Sioux were having a good time.

Crow Bear pointed off to the side and spoke excitedly. All the indians laughed. The Sioux mounted up and sat watching a while. Satisfied their plan would work, they rode away, laughing and talking boisterously as they disappeared into a wide, deep canyon heading toward the Black Hills. The Sioux party dropped quickly down the steep canyon wall which, coupled with their loud merriment, soon put them out of earshot of Early and Josiah.

Jim waited until they were out of sight, then quickly moved towards Josiah. The huge rattlesnake was now coming up on the helpless victim, not yet in position to strike. Jim crawled up to the opposite side of Josiah. "Don't even blink, Josiah. Lay very still. If you move, he'll get you. I'm here. I'll take care of you."

The big rattler glided up near Josiah's head, the black vertical slits of his eyes locked on Josiah's horrified, staring eyes. The snake's black forked tongue flicked in and out of its gruesome looking face. Josiah was paralyzed with fear and hypnotized by this monster who was ready to kill him as if he were a prairie gopher. The desert diamondback was about five feet long. Its thick body, about as thick as Early's arm, started writhing into a coiled position. It was quickly coiled.

With a smooth motion, Jim moved his Colt above Josiah's body. The rattler changed his focus at the movement and looked straight at the small black circle of the end of the barrel as Jim fired. The big body of the snake thrashed around, slapping Josiah's chest and belly, but the head and fangs were gone. Josiah was saved. Jim grabbed the snake's body and threw it away.

Early untied Josiah's hands and feet from the four stakes and Josiah collapsed into his arms. Jim carried Josiah to the shade of a rock and waited for him to come around.

The snake's body still convulsed in the hot sun. Jim had heard that a snake's headless body will do that until sunset on the day it is killed, running on its nerves. He didn't know. He didn't care.

NINETEEN

"JOSIAH, I KNOW YOU'VE been through hell, but we can't stay here with all these rattlesnakes."

Josiah looked scared but he nodded agreement. "Yes, suh".

"Can you make it if we go easy? It's mostly downhill from here to the river and we need to make it back to the others by dark."

" 'Course, Jim. Ah's still 'live, thanks to you. Ah got tired walking back a them hosses in the sun but ma head's cleared up and this bitty bullet hole ain't nothin 'longside that snake." Josiah smiled feebly.

"We have to keep going right now until we're safe back in the cave. We'll stay there tonight and tomorrow and maybe leave tomorrow night. Can you do that?"

"Ah think so, suh."

"You rest here a few minutes while I scout the area to see if there are any more indians around and we'll start back. Better not sleep 'til we're out of the snakes."

Jim started to walk away and then turned back to Josiah. "By the way, you're as brave a man as I've ever seen in war or on the frontier. I'll put in with you, anytime." Pride was in his eyes and Josiah knew he meant it.

Jim scouted from the very top of the snake butte, carefully avoiding a big coiled rattler, sleeping in the sun on a rock about fifteen feet away. Jim was very careful moving around as he went back to get Josiah.

Coming down off the top, Early saw the body of the dead snake still giving an occasional good flop. He thought briefly of taking the snake back to the cave to skin out for supper, but decided it wouldn't be fair to Josiah to cook the snake. Come to think about it, he believed he'd rather go hungry, too. He did stop to collect the leather thongs from the stakes where Josiah had been tied.

Josiah followed Jim down off the butte and they moved cautiously away from the horror they had experienced. Hours later, they were looking over a badlands rim, down onto a grassy plateau. Buffalo grazed below them.

"Must be a spring here, Josiah, buffalo have to have water. We'll go down through here and head out the other side. Just beyond that ridge yonder, we should drop down to the river but I could sure use a drink now, couldn't you?"

"Yes, suh. Man, Ah's dry! Let's go."

Jim thought about trying to kill a buffalo with his little Colt but thought again. He might be biting off more than he could chew with such a big animal - better find the water. Moving across the flat, Jim wondered how buffalo got in here.

At first look, the plateau seemed to be completely ringed by badlands. Except straight ahead, toward the river, the flat did seem to drop off gradually but the ridge before the river was in the near distance beyond and seemed to complete the enclosure.

Off to the side, a cluster of dwarfed evergreen trees grew against the pink striped mud of the badlands hill. "There's the water, Josiah," Early said and veered towards the trees. A buffalo cow and spring calf came out of the trees and walked away. Their muzzles were dripping and their front feet and forelegs were muddy. The cow grunted repeatedly as she walked.

As they entered the shade of the trees, the coolness was a great relief. The spring flowed out of a soft rock layer about two feet above the pool that the buffalo used. They made their way around the pool and both drank their fill of clean, cold water. Then, they lay down in the shade for a rest and both fell asleep.

An hour later, Josiah moaned in his sleep and swung his good arm through the air above him. The old bull buffalo drinking at the pool bellowed, reared and jumped sideways splashing muddy water in a big spray. Jim came up with his Colt in hand and saw the old bull snorting and looking straight at the intruders.

"Easy, partner, we'll just slide out between this tree and the bank, here," Early said. As they disappeared from his view, the old buffalo stood huffing for a few minutes, then went back to drinking water. "Well, I'm awake now," Jim said.

"Me, too." said Josiah. They both laughed and walked out on the flat. They looked back to see the old bull emerge from the trees. He paid no attention to them and swatted flies with his tail as he meandered toward his cows.

"Well, we lost some time but we'll be better off," Jim offered.

A small herd of antelope, that had been lying in the grass about fifty yards away, stood up to look at them. "Lay down, Josiah" Jim said as he dropped on his belly in the grass. He rolled over on his back and waved his arm above him with his pistol in his hand, alternately dropping his arm to his chest to rest. The curious antelope slowly approached. "Lay still, Josiah" Jim whispered.

Within a few minutes, the antelope straggled closer to the two on the ground. Jim picked out this spring's kid and dropped him with a head shot. The rest of the herd jumped and ran, bounding over the grassy flat at high speed.

Early gutted out the small antelope, drained the cavity, and stuffed him with grass. Jim carefully replaced the two spent cartridges in his Colt before he shouldered the young animal and headed for the river.

Dropping off the plateau, they walked down a gradual slope all the way to the river. They didn't have to cross the ridge ahead because the river flowed around this end of the ridge. They walked along the river back to the cave and got to camp just at dark. Mueller and Grant came out of the cave as they walked up.

"Mueller, you're awake!"

"Go straight to hell, Early."

"He's weak, but back in this world," Grant said. "He'll be slow but he should be able to travel tomorrow if we get some of that meat in him."

Jim skinned the antelope and washed it inside and out in the river while the others built a fire and burned it down to coals. They roasted it for about an hour and feasted on the hot meat. Some was burned a little, some a little rare, but the four ate their fill before curling up in the cave to sleep one more night.

TWENTY

Two weeks later, they had covered many miles across the vast prairie and were nearing the Missouri River. They had seen no hostiles nor any dangerous animals. Stands of trees along the Cheyenne River had afforded protection from the hot sun during the days. Nights were starting to get pretty cold. It was harder to move fast enough to keep warm.

Between daybreak and when the sun rose on the prairie each day, Jim scouted out the surrounding country. While he was gone, Grant and Mueller fashioned shelters from downed trees, branches, and sticks. Josiah gathered materials for them as they worked on the shelters.

Routinely, they set up two areas - one for the troopers and one for Early and Josiah. The shelters were designed to be extra protection from the eyes of any marauding Sioux if any came near during the day.

The Cheyenne River had slowed to a steady flow of much less water. There were still deep holes and deep stretches along undercut banks, but often the river was wide and shallow. Small streams still fed into the river but these were sometimes just a trickle. Walking in the river valley at night was difficult as they crossed the surface strewn with stream-rounded rocks.

They were hungry almost all the time and their strength and stamina was greatly reduced. Angry confrontations were common between them. They knew they had to keep going every night or die in this vast, wasteland prairie. When they found berries, they ate all of them wherever found. They washed and ate green plants like dandelions, roots and all.

Just before daybreak one morning they had been lucky to

find a porcupine, which they killed with a stick and skinned out, carefully avoiding the barbed quills. After Jim returned from his morning reconnaissance and declared a small fire should be safe, they roasted the small animal and lay down for the day with full bellies.

On another occasion, under some cottonwoods bordered by scrub evergreens, they were able to kill two fool hens with a stick. These small grouse didn't have a lot of meat but, roasted and cut up, they were better than berries and dandelion greens. Water suitable for drinking was always available from the river or a feeder stream.

After an especially cold night, Jim picked a high spot for his recon. This morning he was very tired when he reached the top. The sun was already up. Sunshine was not in the bottoms yet, but the sun was high enough it didn't blind him as he looked east across the prairie.

Movement caught his eye. A cloud of dust was raised by a single horseman several miles away traveling south towards the Cheyenne River. Jim watched intently. This was, no doubt, an indian. He was too far away to tell for sure with the naked eye. He was no danger to their present position and if he held his course, he would travel away from them all day and be well away by the time the cavalry party moved again. He just needed to be sure that the indian didn't go down to the river and stay in the river bottom.

While the horseman rode slowly, Jim looked over the rest of the country all around. There was nothing but buffalo to be seen. Early sat up, feeling safe here. He wished he had his field glass.

Then, he spotted a coyote trotting toward some buffalo from the base of the butte he was sitting on. The wild dog eventually lay down to watch the buffalo. His hair, in shades of browns and greys, blended with the grasses as he lay perfectly still. When Jim looked away, and then back, he found it hard to locate the coyote again.

Seemed odd this coyote was alone. Ever since the troop had entered Dakota territory, they had heard the staccato, high pitched yelps of coyote packs every night at dusk, even when they were in the Hills.

The sound was spooky at first, but everyone got used to the

evening serenade and scarcely noticed it anymore. In the entire trip no one had seen even one coyote because they seemed to hunt in packs at night and stay out of sight of the moving humans.

The distant mounted figure now rode along the rim of the river valley looking for a gradual descent, then rode over the edge out of Jim's sight. From his vantage point, the scout could see the river and he waited for the horse and rider to appear again. In a short time, the stranger rode into view, dismounted at the river, watered his horse and lay down at the water's edge as if drinking.

Soon, the rider mounted up and headed south again. Jim watched until he was out of sight, breathed a sigh of relief, and headed to rejoin his comrades. This one would be no danger to the little group he was sure. Their paths would cross in the night tonight but the indian trail would be cold.

Jim Early slipped into the trees quietly and was shocked by what he saw. Mueller had Josiah backed up against a tree, one hand on Josiah's throat and his service revolver in the other, shouting curses and threatening to kill him.

New-found strength propelled Early across the short distance and he struck the big sergeant at the waist with a flying leap. Mueller's pistol flew out of his hand at the impact. The two men hit the ground vying for the best advantage as their momentum rolled them over and over downhill until they hit a tree. Jim was on top of Mueller when they stopped rolling.

The sergeant was tiring fast but he bucked Early off before Jim could pin him down. Both men jumped to their feet and Mueller charged like a bull. Jim stepped aside and landed a hard blow to Mueller's face. Blood spurted from the sergeant's nose and he hit the ground sitting with surprise and pain on his face. "Mueller, you son-of-a-bitch." Jim was out of breath but standing with his Colt drawn and pointed at Mueller's forehead.

"You nigger lovin' bastard, Early," Mueller gasped as the blood flowed off his chin. His face was red with rage. Mueller wanted to fight the scout in spite of the Colt, but the steely, unnatural look in Jim's cold blue eyes at the moment convinced him Early would shoot to kill. "You've got the drop on me, Early, but I swear I'll kill you and this nigger, too, before we're through."

"You touch Josiah again, Mueller and you won't live to tell about it. Are you all right, Josiah?"

"Yes, suh. He was jus' startin' on me when you showed up."

Fred Grant walked into the trees coming back from the river as Mueller stood up. "What the hell happened to you, Sgt.?" Mueller ignored him and went to the river to stop the blood and clean up.

"Colonel, settle Mueller down, will you?" Early pleaded. "I didn't see any hostiles around to bother us this morning. Our biggest problem is that we haven't had enough to eat. I'm going to see if I can find something and I'm taking Josiah with me. Why don't you gather some wood and we'll try to have a fire later? We'll be back as soon as we can."

"Come on, Josiah. Are you up to it?"

"Yes, suh."

"Early, we'll be all right here. I hope you can find some meat. We already have the shelters ready for today, so we'll gather a little wood and turn in until you get back."

TWENTY ONE

AN HOUR LATER, JIM and Josiah were making their way up a grassy rise in the prairie when Josiah fainted and fell to the ground. Jim turned him over on his back and Josiah's eyes opened. "Sorry, Jim, Ah'm tahrd."

"That's all right, Josiah. Stay here and rest. I'm going to pull you over here in the shade. How's your arm today?"

"Sore. Feels bettah than it did, though. Gettin' bettah slow, Ah think."

"Good. Stay here. I just want to look over this hill. If I don't find anything, we better start back to the river. Good thing the days aren't so hot anymore."

Jim slowly raised his eyes above the hilltop. He could see a small herd of buffalo fifty yards away, grazing and walking away towards the next hilltop. Jim wished he had his Spencer. He watched as the buffalo went over the top out of sight. He felt weak and very tired. Hunger was with them all the time now. His body was almost numb to the ever present condition.

He still couldn't bring himself to waste his precious few cartridges trying to kill such a big animal with his Colt. A wounded buffalo could turn on him and he would wind up dead. Besides, he didn't have any energy left. Jim rested his chin on his hands and dozed off.

When he woke up, from long habit, he opened his eyes and got his bearings before he slowly raised his head above the hilltop. He couldn't believe his eyes. There, not ten yards away, was a small antelope lying down. Jim lowered his head and backed down enough to get his Colt out without alarming the animal. He crawled into position again and fired. The antelope struggled as if to get up and fell dead.

Jim cut the hind quarters off and tied the feet together with the thongs he had saved from snake butte. Wearily, he hoisted the meat over his shoulders and headed back for Josiah.

When Jim and Josiah got back to the river camp, Jim skinned and washed the haunches. They roasted them and ate their fill before laying down in their shelters for the rest of the day. They all slept soundly until almost dark.

Josiah woke with a start and Jim was instantly awake. They went down to the river to wash up and as they returned to the trees, talking quietly, the others got up, stretching. As Grant and Mueller took their turn at the river, Early cleaned up the campsite and cut some chunks off the second haunch so everyone could eat some and take some along.

The two cavalrymen returned in the twilight just before dark. They stopped, motionless, just inside the trees and stared past Early. As Jim glanced to see what they were looking at, a coyote howled, not ten yards away.

"Move easy, just walk away," Early said. They all backed downstream as the coyote advanced, eyes blazing. The coyote stopped to yip his high pitched howl. Somehow, when being stalked by this prairie wolf, this close, the screeching sound was fearsome ... definitely not a serenade. Early pulled the Colt. A chorus of unearthly yips erupted as the pack appeared behind the leader. "Don't panic. Don't run." Early took careful aim and dropped the lead coyote. The pack hesitated until they smelled fresh blood, then they tore into the downed one in a snarling frenzy. The four men backed away faster and when they were out of sight of the fighting coyotes, they moved away quickly.

"They'll stay busy there a while," Early said. "The rest of the antelope haunch and leg bones are still there, too. Josiah, did you get away with any chunks of meat?"

"Two."

"All right, you can split with me." At that point he untied some meat chunks that he had tied to his waist with thongs and gave them to Grant who shared with Mueller. "Eat 'em now or later," Jim said.

Without much conversation, the men put miles between them and the coyotes, constantly looking back over their shoulders. The coyotes didn't follow. Hours later, a shiver went up everyone's back when they heard the pack howling in the distance.

TWENTY TWO

Two NIGHTS AND TWO days later, the four survivors came out on the broad open valley of the Missouri River. The hungry men drank the muddy water from the deep, wide river. The alkaline taste was unpleasant after the clear water they were used to. They had all become skinny, bearded versions of the troops who had gone to the Black Hills. It seemed so long ago.

After the endless monotonous prairie, the valley of the Missouri in this area was beautiful. Low rolling hills to the horizons, split down the middle by the meandering wide blue river. Yellow-leaved cottonwoods forested the other side of the river almost continuously. On the west side, the trees were divided into dense stands separated by miles of grassy flats and low hills.

The grass was belly high to a horse, brown now, and the cottonwood leaves were golden. When the wind moved the branches, a few leaves fell. So far, the big trees were still dense and the cottonwood stands were acres in size and afforded good concealing cover.

As the men went up the river toward Fort Lincoln, they still travelled at night but each morning they moved away from the river to hide out in the big cottonwood stands. There were always bushes and brush along the edges of the trees which usually included berry bushes.

They saw no buffalo now. They heard no coyotes at night. One night, after smelling smoke, Early scouted out the Sioux village of Crow Bear's people. He guided his group around the village without incident.

Mueller brooded. If he were going to kill Early, he knew it would be best to get the job done before they were back in military jurisdiction. Since their fight, the Sgt. had been withdrawn and surly. He didn't even talk much to Fred Grant and he said nothing to the other two.

On the third morning along the Missouri, the scout came into the large, dense stand that they had picked out in the early light of dawn. He had trouble finding the others. When Jim located the camp, everyone seemed to be asleep. Grant had decided no extra concealment was necessary here. Jim found them sprawled out singly in a small clearing under huge overhanging cottonwoods. He sat down near Josiah, looked around, lay down and went to sleep.

Cold steel against the side of his head woke him with a start.

"Give me your gun, Early," Mueller said in low tones by Jim's ear.

"Not by a damn sight."

Early heard the oiled action click as Mueller cocked his pistol. "Give me your gun, Early."

The scout sat up suddenly and with one arm he forced Mueller's gun hand away so the pistol was pointing at the sky. With the movement, Mueller pulled the trigger automatically but the gun didn't fire. Jim stood up with his Colt in hand and with the business end pointed at Mueller.

"Mine's loaded, Sgt. I've known since the cave that you don't have any ammo. I'm the only one here with a gun that works. Lay your pistol down and go over where you were and go to sleep. I'll give your gun back when we get to station. Don't think I'll forget this but I won't report you because you're half starved and you may be sick from your injury. Go on, get over there."

Mueller was furious but he followed Early's order and lay down because Early was steely-eyed again. Jim tied the extra pistol to a thong at his left side. His buckskin shirt hung over it. Josiah and Grant had both slept through the encounter.

Mueller fumed and couldn't sleep but every time he looked at Early, the scout was watching. No chance to try anything else.

TWENTY THREE

DAYS LATER, AT DAWN, Early climbed to the top of a ridge and saw the most welcome sight of his life. A couple miles up the river he could see the American flag flying at the tip of a very tall flag pole over a U.S. Army fort. The fort was set on a plateau edged by a high bluff above the river. Jim could see a few men on the parade ground as he looked over the stockade walls of the frontier fort.

Early slid and tumbled down from his recon and almost ran to where the others were settling in for the day. Brush whipped Jim's legs and he stumbled over a dead branch as he hurried to give them the news.

Grant instantly saw that Early was not his usual calm self as he came lurching into camp. "What's the matter? What's wrong?"

"Nothing's wrong. Couldn't be better. Old Glory's flying just over the next rise. We're finally safe. Let's go get breakfast!"

The happy men dredged up extra strength from beyond their reserves because their reserves had been long used up. There was a giddy feeling of relief among them as they came in sight of the fort and its flag. As one man, they hurried up the trail to the gate.

At the sentry's challenge, Grant called out "Lt. Colonel Fred Grant, United States 7th Cavalry, and party request permission to enter."

"Hold it right there ... Sir," the sentry added just to be safe. This was about as ragtag a group as the Corporal could possibly imagine - and one was a nigger. Could this possibly be a Lt. Colonel? Still, nothing was too surprising on the frontier. "Just a minute and I'll get the Officer of the Day."

Grant alone was taken to the office where he was bombarded with questions by the commanding officer.

"Welcome to Fort Rice, Dakota territory, Colonel. Looks like you have all been through a lot. Where did you come from? On what orders? Who's with you? The O.D. said one of your men looks like he's a sergeant."

"I am enroute to Fort Abraham Lincoln, assigned as aide to General Custer. It's a long story, sir ... did you say Fort Rice? Where are we exactly?"

"Fort Rice is about twenty eight miles south of Lincoln along the river. Both forts are on the west side of the river. I'm afraid that's where the similarity ends. Rice is ten years old and pretty rough compared to Lincoln - they're at the end of the railroad now and they've imported regular construction materials and professional crews from Minneapolis. Lincoln is brand new, may not be quite completed yet. I'm told they actually have plastered walls. Care for a cigar, Colonel?"

"I'm afraid I couldn't take it right now. I really need a drink but even a taste would knock me on my butt, I'm sure. We all need food. We've been starving for a month or so, lost track of time, but I think we've been out on the prairie a month or six weeks."

"Of course. Listen, Colonel, I'm going to bring you and your party into the fort and feed you and issue you some clothes. We'll get you all past the Doctor for medical attention and billet you for a few days. Then we'll arrange your transportation to Lincoln."

"Thank you, sir. I'll report your good offices not only to General Custer but also to my father, the President of the United States. I appreciate your warm welcome, I'm sure we all do."

"Grant," the C.O. mused. "You say you are Colonel Grant of the 7th Cav and your father is President Grant?"

"Yes, sir." Grant said with a smile. "Right now, breakfast and quarters are our most serious needs. We walked all night last night and every night for a long time."

"Let's get your men and we'll get started. Do you think you can give me a report in the next couple days?" the C.O. asked as they left his office.

"Yes, sir," if not tomorrow, at least by the next day. By the way, what day is it?"

"October 7, 1873, Colonel. General Custer has gone east but I believe he is due back soon. The 7th pulled in from the Yellowstone campaign a couple weeks ago and part of them are here at Rice. Just a minute, sir."

The Commanding Officer turned to a lieutenant and directed him to conduct Colonel Grant's party to the chow hall and see that they were well provided for.

"Yes, sir." The lieutenant left on his way to pick up the others at the gate.

The C.O. took Grant to his own quarters where his gracious wife extended the best hospitality the post could offer their honored guest. Grant slept in a vacant Bachelor Officer's Quarters, ate the excellent meals prepared by the C.O.'s cook, and enjoyed the companionship of the couple in their home.

Josiah was conducted to the kitchen where he was well fed by a colored cook. The starving men in the chow hall, Early and Mueller, found their eyes were bigger than their shrunken stomachs. They grabbed everything in sight but could only eat part of it. Each man had a full loaf of fresh baked bread, salt pork, a bowl of beef stew, and a big tin cup of hot coffee.

"Don't eat too much or you'll heave it right back up and you'll feel awful. Better to just eat some and come back for more later," the Mess Sgt. said. "I'll be here all day."

A sergeant showed up to take them to barracks where they gratefully sacked out for the day and the following night. Josiah was taken to a small building where, it turned out, the cook and a couple other colored soldiers bunked.

In the military setting, after some rest, Lt. Colonel Grant was in his glory. In four days at Fort Rice, he signed for new uniforms for the three soldiers; borrowed horses for himself, Josiah, and Early; and checked out guns and ammo all around. Jim's buckskins had to make do until he got to Lincoln but he used the Lieutenant's razor and felt better right away.

The post surgeon wanted to keep Sgt. Mueller for a week or so to work on infection in his scalp and to get his wound healed up, so Grant authorized him to stay and to come up to Fort Lincoln when he got released.

Everybody got fed and rested. Josiah's arm was still tender but healing well. He would have permanent angry scars for the rest of his life but no lasting functional damage. The remaining three rode away up the river on the fifth day.

TWENTY FOUR

A CAMARADERIE HAD DEVELOPED between the three survivors as they rode to Fort Abraham Lincoln. In the two day ride from Rice, without the pressures of fear, hunger, and Mueller's anger, Grant and Early talked together a great deal and came to know each other better. Grant even tolerated Josiah and talked to him some; friendly but coolly, in the sense that he was the officer and Josiah the darky private. Nevertheless, Josiah felt good about that, and he thought the sun rose and set on scout Early. All were feeling good when they got to Lincoln.

The men turned in their borrowed horses and horse gear at the stables, where they asked directions to the guardhouse. As they walked half the length of the parade ground carrying their rifles, they admired the well-built, brand new post. They thought there had never been such a beautiful outpost, on such a grand scale, anywhere else on the unsettled American frontier. It was almost as though such a fort had been especially created for the flamboyant Custer and his pride, the 7th Cavalry. A fitting field post, too, for the President's son as Custer's aide.

At the guardhouse, the duty Corporal ushered Grant in to see the Guard Officer of the Day and logged in Early and Josiah in the guard room. The O.D. and Grant left the guard office, told Grant's companions to wait for further instructions, and walked briskly back across the parade ground to the adjutant's office. Soon the three officers could be seen approaching the home of Major Marcus Reno, acting Post Commander in Custer's absence.

As Early and Josiah waited in the guard room, Jim checked out the sparsely furnished room. Besides the carpenter-built table and chair used by the Corporal for a desk, there were wooden bunks with hay-filled bedsacks and blankets. The soldiers on the 24-hour duty roster, but not now on post, were allowed to read (if they could) or play cards on the bunks. They were pretty noisy most of the time. Jim and Josiah sat on the edge of an empty bunk.

Opposite them were six locked cells with solid wooden plank doors that had an iron bar padlocked across. There was a narrow slit near the top of each door, Jim guessed it was for guards to communicate with prisoners without unlocking and maybe to allow some heat from the guard room to filter into the cell. Jim guessed these were solitary cells.

In the center of the room there was a gun rack with the guards' Springfield rifles secured with an iron rod through the trigger guards and which was padlocked to the rack. At the end of the room was a large fireplace, the only source of heat against the cold Dakota winter for this half of the long building.

Jim hadn't seen the other half of the building but he guessed it would be a drunk tank where they also held prisoners who had committed minor offenses. Between the two detention areas was an open hallway called a sally port, which ran across the narrow width of the long building. Entry from the outside was only through a door at each end of this hall.

The guardhouse was a frame structure like the rest of the buildings on the new post, but this one was lined throughout with heavy wooden planking for better jail security. The military guardhouse was a better and much bigger jail than the average frontier lockup and was actually the security center for the entire post.

When the O.D. returned to the guardhouse, Lt. Colonel Grant was not with him. Major Reno had deferred Grant's report to be given to Custer whenever he returned to Lincoln, and had assigned Grant to Bachelor Officer's Quarters. The O.D. now ordered Early and Josiah to the quartermaster storehouse to turn in their Ft. Rice rifles and to draw bedroll, mess gear, and clothing. The O.D. said the Q.M. Sgt. would then direct them to their assigned billets.

"Private Briggs, ya won't need a weapon now, but ya'll need an extra blanket where yer goin'. Yer assigned ta bunk in the tack room at the southeast stable. Report ta Sgt. Towers and he'll git ya squared away."

"Sgt., suh, will mah duties be hosses?"

"Towers'll fill ya in, Briggs, but cleanin' stables and forkin' hay ta the mounts'll be part o' what ya do. Ya won't work alone. There'll be fatigue crews and prisoner details there 'most ever' day. Git, Private."

"Yes, suh. Thank yo', suh!"

"Do ya need uniforms...mmm...Early?" The Sgt. glanced at his paper to get the name. "Yer supposed ta git quarters, weapons, and rations, aren't ya? ...and the indian scouts git uniforms, though God knows why. They never wear 'em, at least not regulation."

"I wear buckskins on the trail, but wool would be good until spring."

"A'right, I'll give ya a complete private's clothing issue like I do the indians ... and mess gear and bedding. I'm long on blankets. Tell ya what, I'll give ya an extra blanket, too. These Dakota winters are hell, I hear. What about weapons?"

"Got any Spencers or Henrys?"

The sergeant laughed. "No, just old single-shot Springfield carbines. They all work, but they're old. The military, and 'specially Custer, hold with the theory of long range accuracy rather than how many redskins ya can shoot before ya hafta reload."

"I see there's a town across the river, and a ferry. If I get paid soon, I'll buy my own. I still have a short Colt and I'm due four months scout pay."

"Yer in luck, Early, pay call is day after tomorra on the 15th. I don't know what ta do fer ya fer quarters, though. The barracks're jam-full o' troops. They all got 'bunkies', sleepin' two in a bunk. They's jus' no room fer ya."

"I don't need much, Sgt. Not 'til the snow starts stacking up, anyway."

"Well, I can issue ya a wall tent fer yer own, or, say ... Why don't ya check with 'em Ree scouts north o' the post along the river? Uncle Sam built log houses fer 'em and some of 'em don't live in 'em. They set up their teepees 'round the cabins. Those buildings are big enough fer three warhoops and their squaws and younguns, so they're good size' and they got a fireplace."

"Thanks, Sgt. I'll try the cabin idea. If I strike out, I'll be back for a tent." Early gathered up his gear and headed for the door.

"Look fer Two Strike. He speaks American some and he's hired fer an interpreter. He'd be at the first cabin ya come to."

After carrying all his gear to Two Strike's teepee, Jim missed his bay horse Jube again. Never a day went by he didn't think about Jube and Rose and vow again to somehow return to the Black Hills to kill the bear. If he ran into Cheyenne or Sioux, he would get a few of them, too.

"I'm a scout, Two Strike, like you. I need a place to sleep. Got any room?"

Two Strike was a small indian, compact and trim. He was wrapped in an old blue blanket. Two Strike watched Jim's eyes as the scout spoke, then looked away without answering. Two small indian boys ran out of the teepee ahead of their mother as she came out to tend the cooking fire.

Early waited patiently. Finally, Two Strike gestured toward the cabin and said "Soldier house. My lodge better. Soldier house yours." With that, the indian scout turned abruptly and entered his lodge. Jim walked into the long, low log house. His eyes quickly adjusted to the dim light of the interior.

The cabin had been built of green cottonwood logs, which had twisted and warped as they dried out, leaving many open gaps between the logs. He could see out everywhere, it seemed. Jim had to climb over a big pile of horse gear, hides, military clothing, saddle pads, worn indian clothing and other belongings to get through the door.

There had been a horse in the cabin and the Rees had built fires on the packed earth floor. The fireplace was unused but there was a smoky, dirty smell throughout the big room. Jim set to work cleaning out the manure, the rank smelling hay, and the fire circles to improve the livability.

Early settled his gear in the end with the fireplace, away from the door. He moved some of the Ree storage so the door could close. He gathered fresh-cut hay from the end of the parade ground to pile near the fireplace for a sweet-smelling bed, and he gathered firewood and started a small fire in the big fireplace.

As the fire died down to coals, Jim heard the cook strikers banging evening mess call on the steel triangles outside the three barracks mess halls, all at the same time. Early took his mess kit and went through the chow line at the closest mess hall. He was still in his old buckskins and needed a shave.

When Jim came out, he saw Josiah waiting for him. "Josiah, how does it look for you?"

"A'right, Jim, 'til it gets real cold. They's no fire in the tack room. They's a buf'lo robe Ah can use with ma blankets. Sleep wahm fo' now. Sgt. Towers got plenty wo'k fo' me. How 'bout yo'?"

"See that cabin? That's where I'll be. It needs some fixin' but there's way more room than I need."

"Yeah. Say, yo' gonna buy a hoss?"

"Have to. Why?"

"Sgt. Towers say tell yo' they's sellin' a couple three year old, saddle broke. Nice big hosses. He say come see 'em."

"Tell him I'll drop by in the next couple days and look 'em over."

Josiah legged it toward the stables.

TWENTY FIVE

ON THE 15TH OF October, Jim drew his pay of $30 a month plus forty cents a day for risk and use of Jube and his saddle and horse gear. For four months, he drew a hundred-sixty-eight dollars. Seemed like a lot of money at once. Then he thought how many times he came close to losing his life in that four months and it didn't seem like near enough money. He was better off than the soldiers, even a Sgt. only made $17 a month. The indian scouts drew the same as a cavalry private - $13 a month - but the scouts also got the forty cents horse allowance. Early would get by and have a little to spend in town even though he had to replace all his gear.

After pay call, he bought a tall buckskin mare with black mane and tail from Sgt. Towers. She was a beautiful, sleek horse but Towers said she was "too skittish for the army." He said she was broke to ride but hard to saddle and when you swung up into the saddle you wanted to be ready.

She'd "crowhop pretty good" and trot around nervously before she settled down. She'd "jump straight up with all four feet off the ground and come down stiff-legged ... just jar your guts out."

Sometimes, she would buck a little at first, he said. Then she was a good ride and fast. She wouldn't stand still with a rider up, but pawed with her front foot and edged her rear sideways. Not good for formations.

Towers called her Buck, which he admitted wasn't much of a lady's name, but she wasn't much of a lady sometimes. Early liked this spirited horse. She reminded him of Jube when he first got the bay. He was lucky to find one this good on the frontier. She was worth the twenty bucks he gave Towers.

The sergeant gave him a worn halter with a long lead rope and a bucket of oats in the deal. Towers grinned as Early led Buck away, glad to be rid of "the outlaw" and for good money, too. He hadn't lied to him, the guy was just a glutton for punishment.

The scout staked Buck out behind the cabin and spent a little time rubbing her neck and talking to her in a low, soothing voice. He hand-fed her a little grain and she didn't bite his hand; just blew hard with her nostrils flared, and stretched her neck to reach the grain while standing as far away from Jim as she could.

Buck constantly drew away from his touch, straining against the halter and rolling her eyes. He wouldn't try to ride her for a few days until she was more used to him. He gathered armloads of cut hay from the edge of the drill field and piled stacks around his new horse.

Jim picked up his personal toilet articles at the post commissary. Prices were high on the frontier, everything in the commissary seemed to cost double. He went home, cleaned up and shaved. Still in his worn buckskins, he paid ten cents to ride the dilapidated ferry across the big river to Bismarck. The old boat creaked and strained crossing the swift current but somehow made it to the landing on the other side.

Early stepped off the ferry into a completely different world of hustlers and whores and boisterous, drunken merriment. This shanty town was thrown together to trap the money of soldiers looking for a good time. Of course, he had known it was all here. He had heard the loud music, laughter, drunken shouting and occasional gunshots from the other side, especially at night. Over there, the sound of the river softened the din, and the normal sounds at Fort Lincoln completed the masking effect most of the time.

Women called to Early from a white canvas shack with a painted sign "My Lady's Bowery" and from a rude log cabin called "Dew Drop Inn". Their rouged faces and red lips did little to cover the effects of their hard life. The demands of making a living in their chosen profession, among the tough drunks, exacted its price. He saw "Clark and Bill's Place" and "Mullin and O'Neill Dance Hall" as he strode the dirt street between the little collection of illicit huts.

Jim glanced with curiosity at the people and the buildings as he passed. At this time of day, there were no soldiers in evidence. He saw indians with quick eyes lounging around and a couple drunken civilians arguing.

Jim walked through to the town beyond. He found a blacksmith shop next to a barn that had a crude hand-lettered sign "livery".

"Afternoon," Jim said to the blacksmith.

"Howdy."

"Can you tell me where I might find a decent used saddle?"

"Not 'less ol' Pete's got somethin' in the livery there." The smith didn't miss a lick on the red-hot horseshoe he was shaping on the anvil.

Walking into shade in the barn, Jim couldn't see much. He heard a small noise as something bumped a board and he sensed movement at a horse stall. His Colt half out, he quickly focused on an old man cleaning the stall. Jim slipped the Colt back into his waist. Horses champed hay and the smell of horse manure rose to meet him. Somewhere a horse peed making a hot, hissing sound.

"Pete?"

The old man took his measure. "Who's askin'?"

"Just lookin' for a good used saddle. Fella told me you might have somethin'."

"Fer cash."

"Let's see it." Jim stepped up close and the old man looked at his trail-worn buckskins but he also saw Jim was clean, shaved, and sober.

The old man walked to the back of the barn. He was keeping just four horses, Jim noticed.

"Yonder," the old man said.

Jim examined the saddle. It was almost new, a cattleman's saddle with saddle horn for use in working cattle; and fancy, with skirting and wide leather stirrup straps. Designs were hand stamped all over it and decorative laces hung at the corners. Jim had never had so nice a saddle. His had always been just the plain McClellan cavalry style with smooth pommel in front, always well worn.

"This yours? Where'd you get it?"

"A sharp looker left his horse with me. I boarded him for two weeks 'afore the guy got killed in a poker game at the Point ..."

"The Point?"

"Yeah, Whiskey Point down by the river. Guess he got caught cheatin' and someone didn't like it. I kep' the horse and rig fer the board bill. Already sold the horse. You want the saddle?"

"How much?"

"Fifteen dollars."

"I can go eight."

The old man's shoulders slumped. "I'll keep it."

As Jim turned to leave, Pete had second thoughts. "Twelve dollars, and you get the bridle, saddle blanket, rifle scabbard, rope ... the whole works."

"Ten for everything ... well ... twelve if you'll keep it for me for a day or so. I've got a lot of stuff to buy and the ferry to deal with. Twelve dollars."

The old man smiled a cracked smile. "Safe here as in the bank."

"Thanks, Pete. See you tomorrow. Want the money now or later?"

Pete shuffled his feet and rubbed his grey stubbled chin. "When you get the saddle."

At the general store, Early asked the storekeeper to show him rifles.

"Of course, sir." He handed Jim a Springfield sporter rifle.

Jim hefted the gun without putting it to his shoulder. "Nice balance but I'm looking for a lever action - rather have a carbine." He handed it back.

"Good luck. Maybe someone'll die and ya won't have ta pay for it, either." He giggled a nervous laugh. "Don't get many repeaters here. These Springfields are what everybody wants. They shoot flat at long distance. Much more accurate in the field than a repeater. These are the best for game, even buffalo. They rank right alongside Sharps for buffalo guns. They're basically the same as the Cavalry uses, too. Brand spankin' new for ten dollars. How about it, sir, you can't beat it."

"No, thanks. I will want a box of .44 rimfire but I'm going to pick up a few other things and then settle up for all of it."

Early gathered supplies for his quarters. As he was looking at a kerosene lamp he noticed, out of the corner of his eye, a small sheet iron cookstove on the floor in the corner. The whole thing was basically a firebox on short legs with a loading door for wood in the front, a solid flat top for cooking, and a stovepipe hole in the top at the back. This one was rusty and dusty.

"How much for the old stove?"

"I let a guy have two dollars worth of groceries for it. Said he found it on the prairie back east, evidently kicked out of a settler's wagon. It's good for a lot of fires yet. I'll take three bucks."

"Done, if you got any stovepipe."

"In the back, sir, brand new. Ten cents a foot."

"I'll take ten feet, the ammo, and this other stuff. I'll come back tomorrow for the stove and pipe. I have to carry all of it to Fort Lincoln on the ferry. Have to make a separate trip for the bulky things. Throw in half a dozen of those apples - make sure they're all good ones - and a pound of lemon drops."

Early paid and the storekeeper boxed his supplies in a wooden box. He left the store carrying the box and walked past a well-dressed man sitting on a bench on the board porch. Jim thought he looked out of place in his bowler and suit in this rough town. He had a large, thin, shiny wooden box, like a skinny suitcase with a carrying handle.

"Just a minute, sir. I was in the store when you came in and overheard you looking for a rifle ..."

Jim stopped.

"I tried to sell some new guns to the store but he wouldn't talk to me. He's probably short on cash and he's got some money in his Springfields."

"What you got?" Jim set his box of supplies down and hunkered down beside it.

The drummer opened his sample case on the wooden floor. "I've got the greatest deal in guns you have ever seen. This is the first 1873 model Winchester carbine lever to hit Bismarck, one of the first anywhere - I just got off the train. My friend, this is that 15-shot repeater you need." He handed it to Early.

"Winchester? Almost looks like a Henry." Jim hefted the rifle, levered the action open, and threw it to his shoulder smoothly. He was looking right over the sights perfectly.

"It's based on the Henry. Winchester just bought Henry out ... but this gun is better than the gun the Indians have so many of. This gun has a steel receiver and it's more accurate. Doesn't it have a nice heft and a natural throw? This carbine model is really a greatly improved Henry."

"I've been used to a Spencer but this is a nice light little gun, good balance and in a tight spot you can keep shooting, like I could with my Spencer. In a way, I like this lever better. It's more solid than the Spencer fingertip lever. How much?"

"This carbine is eight inches shorter than your Spencer was. It's a lot lighter and handier. Since I won't have a dealer here, I could give you a deal. This new model is a twenty dollar gun." He paused for effect. Early waited. "I'll let you have it for fifteen dollars if you buy the companion piece, too."

"What the hell...?"

"Here, my friend, is also Colt's brand new 1873 single-action frontier model ..."

"I've already got a Colt."

"I know. You bought a box of rimfires for it, but look at this. There's no comparison between this revolver and your open top '71. This has the solid frame like the '65 Remington. You can use the butt of this piece for a hammer or as a club in a bar fight. Like the new Winchester, this Colt handles better ... and ... it's fast. You can dump it out into a reasonable target in three seconds if you're as good as I think you are. This gun will do it in the right hands."

"Haven't had no complaints but I've had good luck with the Colt I've got."

"One more thing, the 1873 Colt uses the same ammo as your Winchester will, so you only have to carry one kind. Both are chambered for .44/40 centerfire which is the most reliable ammunition available today. What do you think of that?"

"How much?"

"Ten dollar gun." Pause. "I'd like to see you in this new equipment. Your life might depend on it. Eight dollars for the Colt if you buy the pair."

"Thanks for your concern but this is a 7 1/2" barrel. I want a three inch."

"You're tough. This gun is so new, production is mainly geared to the standard barrel. However, I happen to have one special issue I bought for myself with a 3" barrel." The peddler pulled it clumsily from a little holster under his suit coat., shucked out the shells, and handed it to Early. "Twenty three dollars, total."

"What about my good little rimfire?"

"It's outdated, but not everyone knows it. I can move it for five dollars. I'll give you three and I'll trade you a box of centerfire cartridges for your box of shells, straight across. How's that?"

"Deal, and I'll give you another buck for another box of ammo." Early handed him a twenty, a single, and his old Colt. He fished out the rimfires from his supplies and took over his new armament. The drummer slipped the loaded '71 Colt into his little holster, smoothed out his coat, closed his sample case, and headed down the street.

Jim caught the ferry as it was ready to leave. He had his hands full with the rifle and the heavy box, but he was so satisfied with his shopping trip he didn't mind the load. He ate an apple as he leaned on the boat rail. It was heaven.

TWENTY SIX

NEXT DAY, EARLY PAID Pete and picked up his saddle and horse gear. He took them home to store in his cabin. Every time he went in or out, he stopped to talk to Buck. He rubbed her neck and back so she would get used to him and his smell.

Jim took another ferry ride to get his little cook stove and carried it home, setting it down briefly from time to time so he could rest. He wasn't back to his full strength yet.

The storekeeper had charged him an extra fifty cents for an elbow that he could set on top the chimney, facing away from the wind, to avoid downdraft that would fill the cabin with smoke.

Early changed into his military clothing and dug out some tanned skins he had purchased at the store. He approached Two Strike's squaw outside their teepee with his old buckskin outfit and the new skins. He signed that he wanted her to make him a new set of clothes out of the store-bought skins and that he would pay her two extra skins for her work. She signed her agreement and carried everything into the lodge.

Two Strike rode up and as he dismounted, Early pointed to a green hide the woman had been staking out. She also had fresh strips of meat air drying on many long strings.

"Where'd you get this big buffalo hide?"

Two Strike threw the saddle pad off his pony. Letting the long lead rope drag, he slapped the horse on the rear haunch and walked toward Early.

"Rode up to big bull in draw." Two Strike pointed north.

"Shot him five times."

"Would you sell the hide?"

"You bet."

"Five dollars when woman gets it tanned?"

"You bet." Two Strike entered his lodge.

Jim walked to the closest house in officer's row along the back side of the camp. Two of the Minneapolis contractors were still finishing this last house before the last train of the season took them home. Jim went in the back door and asked them if they had any small nails they could spare.

"Raid the scrap pile back of the house. You can have anything out there. The post carpenter has been picking up some things all summer but he hasn't been here for days. Should be able to find some nails. That's junk and we won't be taking it with us." The lead carpenter was cheery since they were almost through with this big job and could soon go home.

A nail keg lay on the other side of the scrap pile. Early set it up with difficulty. It was half full of rusty water. Draining the water off, he found about a third of a keg of two inch iron nails. They were somewhat stuck together with rust but came apart easily and looked to be as good as ever.

Jim made several trips to the cabin carrying salvage including a bag of dry plaster (still about a fourth full), a ragged piece of rusty metal grid, a beat-up hammer head with a broken handle, some usable emptied buckets, wood shingles and scraps of siding boards. He bought a hammer handle and a small saw from the sutler's store and made ready to prepare his cabin for the winter soon to come.

Resting from his labors, Jim soothed Buck with a handful of grain and saddled the nervous mare. He rubbed her neck and talked softly to her, settling her down, while he put the bridle on and slipped the bit into her mouth. He held tightly to the reins and swung up in the saddle. Buck stood stock still.

Early touched her flank with his moccasin heel and Buck jumped sideways and moved off at a trot. Jim reached forward and rubbed her neck and she slowed to a smart walk. "Whoa." As he tugged gently back on the reins, Buck stopped and stood still except for stamping her front foot a couple times.

Jim worked her for about an hour and found her very responsive to neck reining with quick, sure movements. The military training was there, this horse just needed a soft touch to bring out her best. They moved along as one, horse and rider.

Jim rode toward the parade ground. The bugler blew "recall from fatigue duty". He stopped to watch Captain Benteen's boys play a practice game of baseball. They had a few good players but most made up in enthusiasm what they lacked in experience. They were supposed to play a team from Fort Rice on Saturday for the last game of the season. The men liked baseball so well, they wanted to see games until snow fell and many gathered and watched even this practice with great interest. Shouted encouragement and cussin' filled the air.

Early rode back to the cabin, haltered his horse and unsaddled her. He took time to cool her down by rubbing her back and neck with hay, praising her in his soft voice. He hand fed her some oats and went to chow.

Days now were sometimes sunny. Sometimes dark, stormy clouds rolled overhead. Every day was cold enough to see your breath. Early laid his moccasins aside and wore issue boots to keep his feet warm. Rolling up his sleeves, he enjoyed the comfort of the wool government clothes.

Jim worked several long days winterizing his cabin. The scout drove a row of the square iron nails along the bottom edge of the spaces between the cabin logs. He left about an inch of each nail exposed to anchor mud chinking so it wouldn't fall out before spring. Early carried buckets of drained river mud and let it dry to a thick, damp consistency in the buckets. He chinked all the lines between all the logs of the cabin using the thin edge of a shingle for a trowel, sealing out the winter wind, field mice, and next summer's bugs.

The cabin was dark now when the door was closed except for some daylight coming through the fireplace chimney and that was pretty dim. Early set a lighted lamp on his overturned wooden box while he worked inside. He set up his stove in the firebox of the fireplace, ran the stovepipe up through the fireplace chimney, and set the stovepipe elbow on top, facing away from the prevailing winds. Moving his light close, he closed the throat of the fireplace around his stovepipe by shaping the metal grid to the opening and covering the grid over with plaster from the construction salvage. Now, he wouldn't suffer from icy downdrafts from the fireplace chimney every night when his fire died down.

Fatigue details cut wood along the river every day and delivered it to all the buildings on the post with fireplaces. They included Jim's cabin because it was authorized quarters. They also set a water barrel inside the cabin near the door and work details kept it full.

Jim carried the wood in, split it and stacked it in the center of his cabin. "Wood warms twice, once when you cut it and then when you burn it," Jim fondly remembered his old dad telling him when he was growing up.

TWENTY SEVEN

"TRUMPETER'S ASSEMBLY," THE FIRST bugle call of the day on the post, woke Early up fifteen minutes before reveille. The room grew colder by the day. He lit the lamp that was sitting on the box by his bunk and hopped out of his blankets to dress.

Jim started a fire with dried shavings and kindling. His stove was hot and he was warm when the bugler sounded mess call at 6:30. He put on the coffee and made johnny cakes for breakfast. His stove worked well in the fireplace. It got hot fast, didn't smoke inside the cabin, and warmed his living area as well as a fireplace without using nearly as much wood.

Finishing his third cup of coffee, Early decided to give the mare a good workout. He picked up his Winchester, saddled Buck and headed south along the river. It was a pleasant morning as the sun was hitting the valley, warming both horse and rider. Buck's coat was getting shaggy with long hair. She was fat and sassy but rough looking.

An hour later, Jim stood looking across the Missouri, holding Buck's reins loosely. The buckskin dipped her head for a drink. The river was wide here - shallower, with sandbars that looked like stepping stones rising above the water. The other side of the river was off the reservation and considered the "safe side."

Early mounted Buck and urged her into the river. She plunged ahead, swimming as they hit the current. Jim habitually rode with the ends of the reins tied together. As they entered the water, he dropped the reins over the saddle horn and raised his moccasined feet up on Buck's neck to keep dry. He held on to the saddle horn with both hands. They lurched up onto a sandbar and continued across. The big mare was a strong swimmer.

When they rode out on the east side of the river, he dismounted and rubbed her neck and scratched around her ears gently, praising her. Buck shook her head and stamped her feet, spraying water. Early stepped back laughing, "You want me to share the wet."

Minutes after Early started south again, a buck mule deer stood up from his day bed at the edge of the cottonwoods and bounded along the tree line ahead of Early. Jim touched Buck's flank. She didn't need further coaxing to give chase and seemed to enjoy the pursuit.

Jim stopped her on a dime, pulled the Winchester, and dropped the deer with a quick shot. Buck came straight up at the shot and came down hitting the ground on all four feet stiff-legged. She danced around briefly but quickly settled down to a walk.

Jim had nearly lost his seat but he felt good that his new horse seemed to be almost ready for the trail. He would have to work on getting her used to gunfire. This was not bad for the first time.

He gutted out the deer, propped the body cavity open with sticks and washed up his hands and arms in the river. Temporarily, Jim left the deer under a tree. He mounted Buck and headed south again, enjoying the sun, the sound of the river, and the rattling of the bare cottonwood branches, clicking on each other in the light breeze.

Without warning, the horse shied and broke into a fast and jarring trot, throwing her head with eyes rolling. Jim saw something on the ground in a blur as Buck ran by. When he got her whoaed up, Jim tied her to a tree. Winchester in hand, he walked back along the cottonwoods to see what had spooked her.

A white man lay staked out on the ground with no clothes on. He was split with a knife from his pelvis up to the center of his rib cage. White bone showed at both ends of the cut. He had been disemboweled, his guts stuffed back in and a fire burned on top of his guts as they protruded from his opened-up belly.

He squatted down by the scalped, frozen body. The coals were long since cold. Jim judged the man was tortured to death yesterday or the day before but it was hard to tell exactly. For sure it hadn't happened today, he couldn't see any danger now. The Sioux had probably left the body here deliberately to taunt the Fort Lincoln troops.

Jim rode back toward the crossing. He tied the mule deer across his saddle with difficulty because Buck was nervous and prancing. He tied his clothes and guns on top of the deer and led the mare into the icy river. When they reached deep water, he dropped the reins on Buck's neck and held onto the saddle horn, swimming alongside and using the horse's strength to get them across. In the middle of the current, Buck tried to climb on top of Early. He struck her sharply on the nose with the flat of his hand and she straightened out for the opposite bank again.

He put on his clothes and walked the loaded mare back to camp and reported what he had found to the Officer of the Day. He mentioned the convenient river crossing he had found. The O.D. was familiar with it. The 7th patrolled that area once or twice a week but hadn't been there for a couple days.

Early unloaded the deer at Two Strike's lodge. The woman and her little boys came out and Jim signed to her that the meat and hide were hers. Expressionless, she went back into the teepee. The boys ran around playing and shouting.

Jim took care of his horse, went into the cabin, and built a good fire to take the chill out of his bones. He heard the bugler blow "to horse" and, soon after, the clatter and muffled commands of a mounted troop leaving to recover the body and to survey the country there for hostiles. The patrol came back at dusk.

TWENTY EIGHT

As DAWN LIGHTENED THE sky in the east, Jim rolled over in his blankets and looked at the sky above. Cold rain, almost snow, had soaked his blankets - he was very cold and his campfire was out. He heard a faint noise in the timber. Looking across the clearing toward the sound, Early heard a small animal growling noise.

In the gathering dim light, he sat up and reached for his rifle. It was not where he thought it would be. Frantically, he pawed around with his right hand, searching for the gun without taking his eyes off the edge of the timber. He couldn't find it. With loud roars, a huge dark animal ... a giant grizzly ... burst out of the trees running full speed straight at him. The bear was rapidly closing the fifty yards distance from the timber to Early's bedroll.

Early saw his rifle leaning against a tree about ten feet further from the bear than he was. He lunged to his feet, spun around, and tripped on a branch. As he fell, the bear reached him and stood up on its hind legs. Jim was looking straight at the bear's hind feet as he lay on the ground. One foot was missing a toe.

Jim rolled toward the rifle as the bear came down to all fours and roared a horrible, mind-numbing roar. His huge jaws opened. His mouth crashed shut with gnashing teeth, then opened wide as he reached Early. The rifle was just beyond his fingertips as the grizzly attacked. Jim rolled in the mud trying to escape the furious madness, but the bear was nearly on top of him. He could smell its foul breath. The bear bit him and clawed him all over his body. Deep wounds gushed his life blood. Blood spurted in his eyes and everything went dark.

Jim looked down from the tree tops at the scene below as the bear picked up the body by the shoulder and started dragging it

121

away. Blood was everywhere. The body was limp and lifeless and blood soaked. The bear dropped the body and stood up, looked up into the tree tops and brayed his loud challenge.

Jim watched, horrified. The body was Rose. His moan turned into a scream as his whole body ached from losing Rose. The hurt was new again and intense.

The insistent sound of the bugle call woke Early from his nightmare. His blankets were thrown aside and his entire body was bathed in cold sweat. His face was buried in the cold hay of his bed, damp from his breath. Hay stuck to his face and clung to his long johns. Impatiently, he batted at the sticky pieces and reached for his pants. Stark reality banished the cloud of his dream as he shivered and trembled in the cold, dark room. His passionate love for Rose, and his hatred of the bear that killed her, overwhelmed Jim as he hurriedly dressed and started a fire in his stove. He was shaken.

A light snow had fallen during the night. Fort Lincoln and the surrounding country were covered with the white blanket. The crystal blue of the Missouri sparkled as it wound its way out of sight to the south. Buck whinnied as Jim came out of the cabin with a bucket of oats. Jim saddled his mare and took her for a bracing ride to warm her up. He let her have her head and she ran flat out, until, her flanks heaving, she slowed to her brisk walk and they headed home.

Right then, he had an idea for his horse. He thought he'd better see if he could get Sgt. Towers to board her through the winter. Just a little snow and freezing temperature drove home the realization that no man nor beast could survive outside in the deep snow and sub-zero temperatures that were sure to be coming.

Towers said, "Sure. We c'n boahd yer hoss. Ya just have ta pay yer hoss allowance back ta the guv'mint. Ya'll have ta care for her same as always but she can stay 'til spring. She'll be fit and slick when ya can ride her on green grass again. We'll throw her some grain and hay once in a while whenever yo' can't make it, and we'll help with her exercise when we have time."

"It's warming up outside now. I'll keep her another day or two, then I'll bring her in. Don't know if I can get along without her." Jim rubbed her neck affectionately.

"Course, while she's stabled, ya can still ride her any time. Yer not losin' her fer the winter, ya know. She's lookin' good, Early, ya must be gettin' along real good."

"She's just what I was looking for. She's gentled down and she never quits."

"Don't know how ya did it. Couple o' the boys tried to pound some sense in her head but she was too high strung. Good hoss when she was good, but she could be a reg'lar outlaw."

"Don't pound my horse. I'll grain her regular and curry her down like the soldiers do theirs. Matter of fact, why don't you have Private Briggs take care of her if I can't get in. Can we do that?"

"Sure, he c'n work her in sometimes. He's a helluva worker and good with hosses."

"I'll come in most days and take care of her myself but I'll pay for her to eat your grain and hay and stay out of the snow. Anytime the weather permits riding, I'll ride her ... or Josiah can." Jim brushed her mane with his hand unconsciously.

"Boy, I'll tell ya, sure looks like ya got your money's worth, Early. Go to the Quartermaster Sgt. where ya drew yer gear and he's got a paper fer ya ta sign, then ya can leave her anytime yer ready."

"Thanks Sgt. We'll be back. Where's Briggs?"

"He got called ta the ginr'l's house this mornin'."

"The general's house?"

"Yeah, Ginr'l Custer and his Missus got in on the train yestaday. I don't know what he wants with Briggs."

"Tell Josiah I stopped and I'll be back in the next day or two."

Sgt. Towers grinned, waved his hand in answer, and walked away.

Early took his horse home and threw her a stack of hay. When mess call blew for noon, Jim grabbed his kit and headed for the mess hall.

In the early afternoon, Jim walked over to the quartermaster storehouse to sign for Buck's stabling. He could barely get inside the door. The room was packed with troopers. The sergeant was very busy issuing buffalo overcoats and shoes, fur hats and gloves to the men. The troops seemed to be excited about receiving the heavy, warm gear. A holiday atmosphere prevailed. Jim didn't have any place to go, so he stood aside and watched as he waited.

These men were fit and muscled and unusually smart-looking as a group. They knew it and were vain about it, so it was fun for them to see another trooper looking as big and heavy as a buffalo and to tease him. Many didn't try on their new issue to avoid entertaining the company, but picked up the furry load and left to go to their barracks. The ranks thinned out and, finally, the last soldier was gone.

"Belly up ta the counter, Early, and draw yer gear. Yer on my list," the sergeant said with a sigh. He was glad the first group was gone but that was the first of many.

"Looks good to me. What's going on?"

"New regulation outerware for all U.S. soldiers takin' part in the indian wars, as they say. All came in on the train yestaday. It was news to me. Never heard such a thing 'afore."

Early pushed the list back with his signature on the proper line of the winter gear sheet. "I really came in to sign a paper so my horse can be stabled with Towers through the winter. Can I sign that, too?"

"Sure. That'll be the best way ta take care o' yer hoss 'til spring. Here, sign this authorization. Yer hoss allowance'll automatically be deducted from yer pay 'til ya take her back."

Jim read the paper before signing it. A work detail came through the door. "Ya got some ripped tents that'r supposed to go ta the new enlisted men's theater fer curtains?" the Corporal asked.

Jim watched with interest as the detail carried out several tents, all they could carry. As the Q.M. sergeant came back up to the counter from the back of the building, he said, "Damn, there's still one left that they won't need. Got no use for it and it's in the way."

"If you want to get rid of it, I could use it to partition my cabin. I've got it chinked but the room's so big and cold that I have to huddle by the fire to feel the heat. If I could tack some of this canvas up for a fourth wall of my quarters, it would be pretty cozy, I think."

"Ya got it, Early. I'll send it over with a fatigue detail and have 'em bring it in your cabin."

"Thanks, Sgt. I'll buy you a drink at the Point sometime."

"Maybe we could sit 'round a table and swap lies fer awhile."

"I'd like that while I don't have much to do. What's your name?"

"Thompson. John Thompson."

"I'll get hold of you, John; call me Jim."

TWENTY NINE

EARLY DUMPED HIS HEAVY clothing in his quarters; he was a little winded from the exertion but most of his strength seemed to be back. Jim lit his lamp, went back to close the door and glanced outside.

Several of the Ree scouts were gathered at Two Strike's tent. Talking quietly, they were intently looking south along the river. Jim stepped out, closed the door and walked up beside Two Strike. A party of brightly dressed indians was riding toward Fort Lincoln on the near side of the river. Their colorful clothing stood out against the white snow and the sun glinted on their rifles and sparkled on their personal adornments.

"Sioux?" Jim asked.

Without moving his eyes or changing expression, Two Strike nodded yes and answered, "reservation indians. Big trouble maybe."

It would be a while before the approaching party would reach Fort Lincoln - they were miles away along the river bottom. They seemed to be in no hurry, just walking their ponies, but getting closer with every step.

The Sioux were natural enemies of the Rees and these Ree scouts would certainly keep an eye on the advancing party. Jim couldn't see any point in standing around waiting, so he went inside and figured out how he would install the tent material inside his big cabin. He had enough nails and some siding boards that he could split lengthwise to use as nailer strips so the canvas couldn't pull off over the nail heads and fall down. He decided to partition about a third of the cabin to make his living space. That would give him enough room and would be feasible to heat.

Excited jabber at Two Strike's teepee brought Early out again to join the Rees. The scouts were ordering their women and children out of sight. Two were leading all of their ponies behind a rise in the prairie behind Jim's cabin.

The Sioux party was getting close and they were riding past Fort Lincoln, along the river, on a bee-line course for the Ree area. Jim led Buck inside his cabin and tied her by the woodpile. He loaded his Winchester and placed it out of sight inside the door. He checked his Colt and stuck it in the waist of his uniform pants behind the right hipbone. Early positioned himself in the open doorway, leaning casually on the door jamb. He was ready, but would appear to be watching the parley with curiosity as though he didn't suspect any threat from the Sioux. They wouldn't be able to see he was armed.

As the Sioux party came close, their arrogant attitude was plain to see. They were wearing brightly colored wool blanket wraps, and all were ornamented with feathers and shiny dangles. Each warrior held a rifle laid across the front of his saddle pad in plain sight.

Early realized this was a dangerous situation. There were only six Ree scouts, not mounted, standing at their own lodges facing a much larger party of their worst enemies. The fort was nearby but the Sioux could probably eliminate the scouts, including himself, with a single volley and race away before the cavalry could give chase. The troops might catch them but the scouts here, unaided, would all be dead first.

Early recognized the cruel voice and then the face of the leader, who was now slowly walking his horse right into Two Strike, knocking him aside. This was one of the renegades who had left Josiah to the snakes in the badlands. He recognized three others at the front of the pack. Their faces were etched in his memory. He had studied carefully those he could see well at the time.

The lead Sioux was Crow Bear. At this instant he saw Early in the door of the cabin. Crow Bear remembered him as the wide eye who had found the body across the river before the bluecoats came to take it away. He had seen Jim shoot the deer, he had watched him cross the river coming and going. He could have shot this one from his hiding place but he wanted the soldiers to find the body, so he let the white man go to tell them. Now he could shoot him anyway.

Crow Bear did not look directly at Early. He would kill the little Ree to signal his war party to begin firing, then he would turn to the white man. Crow Bear's horse reared in the excitement of the confrontation and it took him a minute to settle the pony down. Two Strike, on the ground, shielded his face with his left arm because he thought the Sioux would run over him with his horse.

Crow Bear turned his pony in a tight circle and came around with his rifle pulling down on Two Strike. Jim's new Colt barked and a blank look of disbelief took over Crow Bear's features. Blood ran down his face from the hole in his forehead and his rifle dropped. Crow Bear's horse bolted and the dead Sioux slid to the ground.

Fanning the hammer on the new Colt, Early took out two more of the renegades from the badlands who were right up front. The Rees dropped their blankets revealing that they were armed as their rifles came up. One of the scouts got the fourth renegade before Early could get to him.

The Sioux party's ponies reared in fear of the gunfire and the smell of blood. The fifteen remaining Sioux headed south, firing back over their shoulders as they fled. Mounted Ree scouts came down the hill leading horses for the six by Two Strike's lodge and they all gave chase.

As the Sioux passed the fort, a couple trooper shots rang out. One shot struck a warrior but he clung to his pony and rode away. The indian fight had happened so quickly, there was no general alarm on the post yet, shots came only from a few soldiers who were near the river path.

The Rees, hot on their heels, exchanged shots with the raiding party riding at breakneck speed. The fleeing Sioux shot four Rees off their horses. The pursuers also gunned down four Sioux and then pulled up. The battle ended with the Sioux in complete rout.

Jim didn't ride with the Rees but stayed at the cabin watching the running fight down the valley. Two Strike's little boys ran out of the lodge crying and scared. Their mother, coming out of the lodge entrance, screamed. One of the downed Sioux raised his rifle to shoot a boy. Early was faster and the Winchester made its first kill.

Early checked the four bodies. They were all dead now. The last one he killed was the one originally shot by the Ree. This was sweet revenge for Josiah's ordeal. Two Strike's wife, crying, gathered up her sons and went back into her lodge.

The Ree scouts came back with two of their own dead and two not seriously wounded. They proceeded to scalp the eight dead Sioux. Jim wasn't sure if the other two from the badlands were here or not. Could be but might not be. He just couldn't be sure.

Two Strike dropped his pony's lead rope outside his teepee, jumped to the ground and disappeared into the lodge. As Jim watched the victorious Rees celebrating the decisive defeat of their mortal enemies, Two Strike immediately reappeared with his family and approached the white scout.

They all seemed happy and smiling but some tears ran down the cheeks of Two Strike's woman, betraying the intense feelings of the normally impassive squaw. She grabbed Early in a warm, impulsive hug of gratitude for saving her husband and her son from the hated Sioux. Jim squeezed back as she held him in a long embrace, chattering unintelligible Ree.

As she let go of Early, Two Strike stepped forward and seized Jim's right arm just below the elbow with his left hand. In return, Jim grasped Two Strike's arm with his right hand completing the strong grip of mutual respect and friendship. Two Strike drew a sharp knife and made small, bleeding cuts in both their forearms at opposing places. The men turned their forearms and pressed the two small wounds together mingling their blood.

"Brothers," Two Strike said.

Jim nodded, knowing that the indian scout would consider him a part of his Ree family forever. The little boys hugged Early's legs and grinned up at him. He picked out two lemon drops from his pocket for them and they were his adoring friends.

Two Strike's wife went back to their lodge and returned with the big buffalo hide. Jim spread it out and admired it. The tanned side was soft and supple. This old bull's hide was especially heavy and would make a welcome addition to his bedroll. The Rees would not accept the money Jim offered. They insisted he take the skin as a gift.

THIRTY

EARLY WOKE UP AT reveille. The cabin was very comfortable with the canvas wall in place and the heavy buffalo robe added to his blankets. He dressed and opened the door to a bright, white glare that briefly blinded him. Startled, he sucked in deep breaths of ice cold air. Four inches of new snow covered everything and it was still snowing. With no wind, the snow fell straight down in big flakes.

Early went to morning mess. After breakfast, he brushed off his horse, saddled her, and took her down to the stable.

General Custer sent the scout word that he wanted to see him at 10:00 for a military briefing. Early shaved and cleaned up, brushed his uniform off and attached the special scout insignia he was supposed to wear. Custer was known to be a "by the book" officer, hard disciplinarian, and hard on troops for the smallest infractions.

Early was shown into the general's library on the main floor of his huge home.

"Mr. Early, sit down and let's begin," Custer greeted him curtly. "I am very upset with reports I've had that we have lost an entire 7th Cavalry troop unnecessarily ... in a chance encounter with Whirlwind Horse's Cheyennes ... in the middle of a congressionally set aside reservation of treaty ... far from that company's route, on orders to join my command at this post."

The General spit his words forcefully in a continuous stream, with pauses for emphasis, and his pale blue eyes glared at Early from beneath his imposing brow and from above his rather long nose and bushy mustache. He stood up and paced in front of Early.

"Sir ..."

"I'm not finished, Mr. Early. I will give you time to speak." Custer cleared his throat and continued. "There was never a finer officer in this command or any other than Captain O'Meara. We fought together in the war and his service record is impeccable ... his bravery and judgement beyond reproach or question. I would have entrusted my own life at his disposal. If he were not surrounded in an impossible, indefensible position ... facing a totally numerically superior armed enemy ... I would have bet my life on his ability."

"It was foolish and indefensible ... indefensible, I tell you ... that this fine officer and his lieutenants and sixty fine men of my 7th Cavalry were ordered to cross the reservation in only company strength. That troop was delivered into harm's way ... yea, to the death ... for no good reason as far as I can tell." Custer's visage was grim.

"I sent strongly worded inquiry to General Sheridan and the Division of the Missouri Headquarters in Chicago as soon as I learned of the loss of these men a few days ago."

"General Sheridan has assured me by wire that official orders for O'Meara's command, of which you were a part, were to proceed right up the Missouri River to report to this post. There seemed to be some intimation, however, that there were unofficial orders to pursue the course taken. I will personally not rest, sir, until this entire matter is exposed to scrutiny. We must not allow any other hapless company to be annihilated in the same way. This matter is not concluded." Custer's face was flushed red as he sat down in his chair again facing Early.

General Custer sat silent, staring through the scout for what seemed a very long time. Early waited. In a completely different tone, Custer continued, "Having apprised you of my strong feelings about the loss of the troop, let me hasten to say, sir, that I have been extremely impressed - I say, extremely impressed - by the flattering reports I have received concerning your own exemplary conduct throughout O'Meara's campaign and last battle. You displayed great ability in delivering your small party of survivors to the eventual safety of this post."

Taking a breath, Custer continued, "I have commended you by name, Mr. Early, to the notice of the President of the United

States through General Sheridan with my official report. I have also recommended to Lt. Colonel Grant that he cite you in a like manner to the President, as the Colonel did to me."

"Let me say, too, that I have not yet received a report from Sgt. Mueller who survived with you. I understand that he, too, dispatched his share of Cheyennes and that he also endured in the face of adversity. I'm told that the two of you had some animosity between you - which is understandable in the circumstances. I do not consider that to be a blemish or a mark against you in any way."

"Now, you have further demonstrated your remarkable military worth to my command by single handedly turning a threatening Sioux movement against my Ree scouts, turning it to a disorderly retreat by those renegades with almost a fifty percent loss to their numbers."

"Further, I'm told you are the one who discovered the citizen's body across the river, and reported it to the post, so a troop might undertake a timely investigation and remove the body."

"I congratulate you, Mr. Early, and personally welcome you to Fort Abraham Lincoln. I am delighted to have you with the 7th Cavalry. I look forward to having you serve with us in the field. Please give me your impressions, now." Custer sat back in his chair looking expectantly at the scout in front of him.

Early took a deep breath. "I'm embarrassed, sir, to receive such strong acclaim from a field grade officer of your stature and reputation. I have heard of your abilities and accomplishments for years. I can only say I am deeply grateful that you are so complimentary and that you have taken time to talk to me in this way."

"May I say that much of the credit for the Sioux engagement certainly should go to Two Strike and the rest of the Ree scouts for their coolness and capabilities in the face of a fierce enemy in a very dangerous situation."

"Yes, I agree. Those scouts were with me all summer on the Yellowstone campaign. I never found them wanting. I am especially fond of Bloody Knife who is half Ree and half Sioux and is my indian chief of scouts. Have you met him?"

"No, sir, I haven't."

"He has been gone to the Arikara reservation north of here since we returned from the campaign. He should be back now or returning shortly. Please continue."

"I certainly agree with everything you said about Captain O'Meara and his troop. I, too, think going to the Black Hills was foolish but I was not privy to the reasons. I got the impression that maybe we were ordered there for a secret reason that was important to the general government. Captain O'Meara said as much to me once when I questioned him pointedly about crossing the reservation in violation of treaty."

"I don't have much to say, General, that you don't already know. I would very much like to offer my praises for the bravery and endurance under impossible conditions by Private Josiah Briggs. He was Captain O'Meara's orderly ..."

"Yes, I know," Custer interrupted. "I have already interviewed Briggs and have arranged for him to serve as my own striker while we are here at the post this winter. He will stay in the servant quarters upstairs with my wife's cook and some others. They have separate rooms. It will be warm there."

"Great, sir. By the way, I would like an explanation of something I've wondered about."

"Go ahead."

"Why was Captain O'Meara's troop not with the rest of your regiment on the Yellowstone this summer but just joining you at the end of the campaign?"

"You know the 7th was on police duty in the south enforcing the reconstruction after the war?"

"Yes, sir."

"Well, when cavalry was needed here to control the indian problems, the 7th was all immediately available except Captain O'Meara couldn't leave until his unit was replaced. His company was several months behind us coming up the Missouri."

"... and Grant?"

"The colonel had been stationed on the Texas frontier for a short time when the decision was made to attach him to the 7th as my acting aide. As far as I know, it was happenstance that he was coming through with O'Meara's company - just worked out that way."

"I see. Do you have any further questions for me?"

"None, Mr. Early. I'm very glad you're with us. If there is anything you need, please let me know."

"Thank you, sir, it's a pleasure to serve under you. My six month's scout hitch is nearly up. I'll re-up with the First Sgt. Also, I want you to know I've got a new horse, and I'm ready to go any time you need me."

"Thanks, Early. Would you like a private conversation with Pvt. Briggs while you're here? He thinks highly of you and Captain O'Meara."

"Yes, sir, I would."

General Custer opened his office door and summoned Josiah from his place by the stove in the parlor across the hall. "Make yourself comfortable, take as much time as you like," Custer said as he closed the door.

Early clasped Josiah's hands in his own, then clapped him on the back. "So, you're in the house for the winter?"

"Yes, suh. Not gonna git cold in the ginr'l's house." Both Early and Josiah laughed. Jim pulled the general's chair away from his desk and sat in it across from Josiah who sat in the other chair. After all they'd been through together, they found it hard to believe that everything was so good now.

"What will your duties be, Josiah?"

"S'posed to keep wood stacked and stoves full; help Mary in the kitchen - dat's Miss Libby's cook; bring his hoss up when he wanta ride. Hafta be ready case the ginr'l want somethin' - 'course he don' need much in winter, they's not much army work. Most time he writin' in hyar or he play pool wi' Miss Libby upstair. Won't let nothin' bother him then. He let me go at supper time. Ah has to be hyar when he come in for breakfas'. Not hard job, Jim, lazy nigger work."

"But boring I'll bet. I'm glad General Custer made you his striker, don't get me wrong. Be nice if you could read so you could use all this time to your advantage."

"Yo know, the ginr'l be fixin to teach the Missus housemaids some readin'. They folks let 'em come hyar but dint want 'em missin' school, so ginr'l he gonna teach 'em afternoons."

"Would you take to that if General Custer would let you in the class?"

"No reason he wud," Josiah sighed.

"He might. If he asks you, I sure would like to see you do it."

"Oh, sure wud if'n he give me a chance!"

"Josiah, you're a free man now. What are your plans?"

"Stay in the army, Jim. Black man can be a man in the army an' they feeds me and pays me to be hyar."

Early thought about Josiah's answer. "I think you're right. Stay away from these wild towns and bars and whores. Learn to love the country and find peace in riding a horse out away from the so-called civilization. Watch out for indians, though. ... say, did you hear we got even with four of those Sioux who led you around the badlands and threw you to the snakes?

Josiah shuddered at the memory.

I'm sure about four. There were eight dead the other day. Maybe the other two were among 'em but I just couldn't be sure."

"There is a way you can help yourself here while you're in the general's house with time on your hands. The English language is not better spoken anywhere in this country than it is in this house. General Custer's a West Point man - even writes for newspapers and magazines. Pay attention to conversation here. Listen to what he and his guests say and how they say it. Practice forming words like they do. Practice, practice, practice silently all the time. Free man doesn't need to talk like a slave. You're already looking good, clean and sharp."

"Ah'll try."

"Make a game of it, Josiah, you'll do fine, like always. This is just a different job, one you can do for yourself. By the way, any time you're around the stables, look in on Buck for me, will you? She likes to have her neck rubbed and her head scratched around her ears."

"Course Ah will. She's a beauty."

"You can ride Buck, after she's used to you, anytime you want. Well, I better go. It's been good to see you. Take care of yourself."

"Sure will, Jim, you too."

Josiah went back to his post. Early asked General Custer if he could have another word with him.

"Yes, Early."

"Sir, there is something I'd like to ask of you. Josiah says you're going to teach Mrs. Custer's housemaids to read. Would you consider including Josiah?"

"Hadn't thought about it. Do you think he'd be interested?"

"Definitely."

"I'll see to it then. I'm always glad to see someone trying to improve himself, especially someone in my command."

"Thank you, sir."

Early left the big house, wading through snow in his winter issue boots and pulling his cavalry dress cape close around himself. He noticed that the guards on posts weren't wearing their buffalo coats yet. It would be that cold soon enough. Heavy gloves and boots and fur hats felt good already.

THIRTY ONE

EARLY PAID FOR A bottle of whiskey at the bar. The bartender set up two glasses from under the bar that weren't too clean. He gave them a quick swipe with a dirty towel and shoved them over next to the bottle.

"You boys lookin' to have a little fun?"

Early shrugged his shoulders, picked up his whiskey and walked away from the whore toward a small empty table. John brought the glasses.

"Who are Mullin and O'Neill, John?"

"Well, that's Dave Mullin with the beaver hat halfway down the bar talkin' to the other bartender. Pretty fast with his gun, I hear. Here's to ya, Jim."

Jim raised his glass and tossed down his shot. Fire burned a trail down to his gut and his eyes watered trying to put out the fire. "Damn," he said softly. "Been a long time. Never was much of a drinker."

"Never did see O'Neill," John poured a couple more shots. The glasses sat there while both men let the glow from the whiskey spread. "This dance hall is more commonly called the 7th Cavalry Saloon in our circles. The boys like it here. Mullin don't allow no trouble and they do have a piana player. Most of the dancin' is done in the back room."

Across the room, Mullin laughed out loud, tipped his hat back and moved on down the bar. Early saw a horse soldier going through a doorway into the back with the woman from the bar. She was looking up at him in a tired way as she closed the door.

Jim shuddered and downed the second glass.

John chuckled. "Post surgeon prob'ly has a few 'old nick' patients from the lovin' at Whiskey Point."

Loud swearing came from the back room. The door was kicked open with a crash as Mueller came staggering into the front dragging a different woman by her arm. She was crying and had red marks on her face from the beating.

Mueller didn't see Early as he stumbled to the end of the bar. "Gimme a drink." Mueller threw half a buck down on the bar. The woman was pounding on Mueller's back with her free fist and cussing him out, but he paid no attention.

"No drink." A man's hand reached past Mueller and pushed the money back to him. Mueller let loose of the whore and turned to Mullin. The woman scurried away into the back room.

"You're new here. I don't want no fights and no beatin' up on ma girls. Ya can leave now and come back when ya want some fun and can behave yourself. Ya got a snoot full now, Sarge." Mullin's right hand rested on the butt of the pistol which he wore on his hip in plain sight. Mueller sullenly looked over the well-dressed intruder. "Just who the hell are you?"

"The sign outside says Mullin and O'Neill's Dance Hall. I'm Mullin. Get out, Sgt. and don't come back tonight." Mueller's face reddened. The bartender had a revolver in his hand resting on the back edge of the bar. It was pointed at his belly button. As Mueller backed away toward the door, the bartender replaced his gun on the little shelf just under the bar and poured a whiskey for a customer.

Mueller bumped into an empty chair which made a loud scraping noise on the bare wood floor and he stumbled. "Damn it to hell." Mueller kicked the chair over and it flew smashing into the wall.

Mullin's gun hand moved slightly.

"No," Mueller said. "I'm leavin." He went outside into the cold night and the bar noise gradually came back to normal.

Mullin was on edge now. Hands on hips, he stood by himself midway between the bar and the door. A shot rang out from the other end of the bar. Too late, the right hand closed on the gun butt as Mullin fell to the floor. A small dirty white man, gun in hand, sidled to the door and quickly slipped out. The piano player quit playing.

Both bartenders came out from behind the bar and kneeled by Mullin. Blood poured from his chest. His eyes glazed and he thrust his chest upwards in a dying spasm. Early and Sgt. Thompson found themselves in the circle looking down on the dead man.

"Early, you sonuvabitch, here's yours." Unnoticed in the excitement, Mueller had come back in and now stood at the back end of the bar with the bartender's gun pointed at Jim.

"Mueller, you're drunk. There's been enough killin'. Put it away." Nobody moved, the room was silent.

Mueller grinned evilly, drunkenly, as he savored the position of power he was now in. "Early, I've waited too long to rid the army of you, you galvanized-yankee scum. The boys in blue missed you during the war, you reb bastard, but I won't. His finger tightened.

The whore laughed as she came out of the back room with the trooper. Drunken Mueller automatically glanced at the sound and his right hand blew up. The bartender's pistol skidded across the floor. Blood and bone and bits of tendon flew all over Mueller and the bar, and the big mirror on the wall behind him shattered into jagged shards. Mueller passed out from the shock and slumped to the floor. Early stuck his Colt back in his waist.

"Damn, Jim, never seen anythin' so fast! Thought you was a goner. How the hell can you hit what you're shootin' at from under the table?" Thompson was bewildered.

Several cavalrymen approached the downed sergeant. He was not dead but bleeding badly from what was left of his hand. They used a bar towel for a tourniquet and another to wrap the broken, bloody hand.

"Better get him over to the post surgeon," Early said. "He'll live but he'll have to learn to shoot left handed." The troopers were white faced as they picked Mueller up and headed for the ferry slip. Light snow was falling and it was getting very cold. Early and Thompson returned to their table.

"Everybody out. This bar's closed," the bartender shouted above the noise of the crowd. No one paid any attention to his repeated orders. He picked up his pistol off the floor. It was useless now, frame bent from the bullet's impact.

The bartenders talked. "I feel bad," he told his partner. "Dave was a good boss, he was just trying to make a livin'. That weaselly little sonuvabitch is the drunk Mullin threw out last Sat'day night."

"Yeah, I know. This was the first time he'd been back. I wouldn't serve him 'til Mullin give the go ahead. We shouldn't of. No one figured him fer a killer. It wasn't right. Dave didn't have a chance. Ah'll tell ya, I'm through bartendin'." With that, he left to get the undertaker for Mullin.

The remaining bartender moved to his partner's station to be where the other pistol was hidden under the bar. He was uncomfortable looking across the bar at his dead boss on the floor, so he moved the gun to his own station and tried to ignore the body.

The piano player walked nervously up to the bar. "Pay me, I'm leavin." The bartender reached in the till for the usual two bucks and the piano man hurried out.

"When ya gonna clean up this damned mess?" a man that looked like a rancher demanded.

"No use. I tried to get you damn rummies outa here. When yer all gone and the undertaker gets poor Dave, we'll close her up."

"Fer good? Where's the other owner?"

"As far as I'm concerned - fer good. O'Neill went back east with a whore right after this place opened. Dave bought him out. O'Neill did'n have the stomach fer the business. Now, Dave's gone too. Ya know, don't ya, there's no sheriff in Bismarck right now. So, what can we do?"

"How you bartender's gettin' paid?"

"What's it to ya?" The bartender paused, then shrugged. "Actually, Dave paid us every night after work, so we just got tanight comin'. We'll prob'ly split the till, take a jug apiece, an lock the door. No point in cleanin' up the blood."

"Why don't ya buy us all a round, then?"

"House'll buy a round if you sonsabitches'll all move on down the street then," the bartender shouted. Everyone heard "free" and lined up at the bar except Early and Thompson.

Jim Early and Sgt. Thompson had been talking quietly, their glasses empty on the table. "I don't know if I like drinkin' wi' ya, Early. Y'are a rowdy drinkin' pardner."

"Nice quiet evenin' went to hell, didn't it? Well, I've had about enough excitement for one night. Let's have another little touch and catch the next ferry." Jim poured a short one in each glass and pushed the bottle away, still over half full. "Here's to ya, John. Sorry my past caught up with me tonight and ruined our socializin."

They touched glasses. "I'll drink to ya, Jim. Waren't your fault. Strictly legal defendin' yerself. Ya did'n even try to kill this troop. Ah got the feelin' ya shot fer the hand and that if ya was tryin to kill him, ya would've. He called ya - he's lucky to be alive."

As Early and Thompson got off the ferry at Fort Lincoln, a squad of armed troopers were waiting.

"Jim Early?" the Corporal in charge asked.

"Right here," Jim answered.

"You're under arrest, for shooting with a firearm, a U.S. Army Sergeant of this command at Whiskey Point tonight. You'll be held in the post guardhouse in maximum security pending an officer's inquiry. You'll be taken before General George A. Custer tomorrow for review and an inquiry date will be set."

"This is a put-up deal, Corporal. Mr. Early acted in self defense. I was there. That sergeant was drunk and drew down on Jim, without no good reason, meanin' ta kill 'im. Early couldn't a done nothin' else 'cept ta die where he stood."

"Tell it ta the general. My job is ta lock this man up and ta make sure he knows why. Mr. Early, would ya like ta pick up your bedroll at your quarters?"

"Yes." Turning to Sgt. Thompson, "John, will you make a report on this so General Custer will hear it from someone besides me?"

"A'course, Jim."

A trooper searched Early and took his Colt and unloaded it. "Ya bin drinkin', Mr. Early?"

"Yes."

They handcuffed his hands behind his back and marched him to his cabin. Two Strike came out of his lodge to see what was going on.

"Watch my gear for me, will you Two Strike? They're locking me up for shooting a trooper in town tonight."

"You bet. Anythin' else?"

"No, just take care of my stuff until I get back. Maybe just a few days. He tried to kill me for no reason."

"You bet."

"Let's go, Early, we've got your bedroll." The guard detail marched him away.

THIRTY TWO

Jim DIDN'T SLEEP MUCH in the solitary cell that night. It was dark and cold with just a small bar of dim light, and no heat as far as he could tell, coming through the door slit. The wooden bunk didn't have a bedsack and was very narrow and uncomfortable. His warm buffalo robe and two blankets helped some.

The idle guards, whiling away their duty time, were noisy all night. They were especially noisy every two hours when they changed the posted guard - new guard going out, then old guard coming in stomping snow off and shouting at each other.

Every hour, he could hear the sentry's shouts of "all's well" around the posts. Normally, the calls gave a comfortable feeling of security on the post. To a prisoner, they were further invasions of inner feelings.

The guards had shoved him around roughly and swore at him when they had put him in the cell. Treating him like a criminal, a threat to soldiers, they had made him stand in the cell in the dark with his hands cuffed behind his back for a long time before the Corporal came in and took his cuffs off.

The Corporal slammed the cell door as he went out and Early heard the door barred and locked. The cell seemed very small and confining, almost pressing in on this man who loved his freedom of movement. His arms ached from being handcuffed.

After the two o'clock guard change, Jim's eyes closed and he dropped off to sleep. The black darkness in the cell gathered into the ominous form of the huge bear and he was instantly awake as the grizzly bore down on him in a vicious attack. Even here. Nothing could push the bear out of his thoughts.

Early dozed off again just before mess call woke him with

a start. A little later, he heard someone unlock his cell door. A trooper entered and handed him a loaf of yesterday's bread and a tin cup of warm, black coffee. He sat up on the edge of his bunk for breakfast as his cell door slammed shut again.

Later, two soldiers came in and snapped a handcuff on one wrist. "Exercise time, killer," one said. They led him out into the guard room and placed his other cuff around the wrist of a civilian prisoner. Then, all the prisoners were led outside into the awful cold.

All the guards were wearing their buffalo coats now but the prisoners had to move around to keep warm, tromping a path in snow that was over a foot deep. It was snowing and blowing hard, a regular plains blizzard. Early still had his winter issue boots, gloves and hat but most of the other prisoners didn't. The civilian manacled to his wrist was lightly clothed.

He could see in the slowly brightening morning, but just barely because of the storm, the guard mount for the new day forming up on the parade ground. It was almost eight o'clock. The prisoner "exercise" was a mandated morning ritual like the daily guard mount.

"What ya here fer?" Jim's prisoner partner asked through chattering teeth.

"Shot a sergeant at the Point last night," Jim replied. "How 'bout you?"

Involuntarily drawing back slightly, the civilian looked him over.

"Self defense," Early added.

"Got caught stealin' grain from the big granary here. These soldier boys take a dim view o' that. I'm sentenced to six months in this hole. Tryin' to figure how to get away. Ya'll be headed for the Federal pen, they won't keep ya here. Ya should get away now. Maybe we could work together?"

Early shook his head. "Where you goin' in this weather?"

Resigned, the civilian changed the subject. "Ya go before the man today, then?"

"Supposed to."

"All right, you men, knock off the chatter," a guard said. "Time to go back inside and get warm."

Someone opened the outside door and the prisoners filed into the sally port, stamping their feet and shaking snow off their clothing. A guard stood just inside the door directing each man to the proper guard room with a shove on the shoulder in the right direction.

The civilian momentarily lost his balance and the handcuff bracelet bit into Jim's wrist at the unexpected tug. Jim grabbed his arm and helped him straighten up.

"Bastard."

"Careful," Jim said as a guard unlocked the grain stealer's bracelet and led him away. The door slammed behind Early as he was shoved into his cell. Jim rubbed his chafed wrist.

Two hours later, a new Corporal and prison chaser detail escorted Early to the general's quarters, left two to guard him and marched away. The guards uncuffed Early and took positions in the hall on either side of the library door.

General Custer motioned Early into his study and closed the door. Jim stood stiffly facing the general as Custer sat down at his desk.

"At ease, Mr. Early. Tell me what happened."

"Happened very quickly, sir. Not much to tell. Mueller came up with a bartender's gun in the dance hall at the Point and called me."

"He had the drop on you?"

"Yes, sir. I had seen him earlier but I thought he was gone. I was just having a drink with a friend, minding my own business, when Mullin got blindsided and killed. Everyone was watching that for just a couple minutes."

"Mueller was drunk and came back in the bar when my back was turned. He called me. He was distracted by a noise at the back door and I shot the gun out of his hand."

Custer tugged at his mustache in silence for a few minutes. "I've heard from Sgt. Thompson already and another sergeant who was there. I trust both these men. They told me the same story. They said Sgt. Mueller fell to the floor unconscious and you asked some troops to bring him to post hospital. That right?"

"Yes, sir."

"I tend to believe you, Mr. Early. However, as commanding officer, I must set an officer's inquiry. You are a government employee not subject to courts martial as such. This inquiry amounts to the same thing, though, - possible penalty could be a long term in Federal prison. You can't shoot a 7th Cavalry trooper for any reason without facing the possibility of consequences. You will be either convicted or cleared by a panel of officers of this command. I can't do that alone in a matter this serious."

Custer moved a paper over and grabbed his pen. "Sgt. Mueller will face courts martial charges of the same gravity. I'm going to set both your trials about six weeks away so Mueller can recover - I want the same officers to consider both cases at the same time. I will set your inquiry and his court both to be heard on February 9, 1874. Meanwhile, you will still be under arrest - I'm sorry, sir."

General Custer paced. "There is another matter I must bring up with you.

When you turned in your personal belongings from your pockets to the O.D. at the time of your arrest, among the regular things we expect was an unusual item. There is a gold nugget among your possessions ... Tell me ... did that come from the Black Hills?"

"Yes, sir."

Custer's face looked carved from stone. "Tell me about it. Why have I not heard about this before?"

"Because, I just found it there after we camped in the Hills and I had no idea it would be of interest to you. I stuck it in my pocket for a lucky piece."

"Mr. Early, there is considerable interest in this country, particularly in Washington, whether or not there may be gold in the Black Hills. It's been rumored for some time. That area is in the Great Sioux Reservation, which is important to the Sioux, but the President and the Congress of the United States want to be kept abreast of significant discoveries - for future reference should more treaties become necessary.

The Fort Laramie treaty was entered into without our government being aware of what resources might be located within the boundaries of the lands. There's a Catholic priest, a Father DeSmet, who's been telling anyone who'll listen that his 'children', the Sioux, have gold in their possession that they claim comes from the Black Hills.

He has different stories that he always tells 'in confidence', hoping that the information doesn't become public, because he fears a white invasion that would forever displace the indians. He tells just enough to foster big rumors which are sure to generate the interest he says he wants to avoid. The general government would be interested in confirmation of definite findings there."

"I don't have 'findings', General, just the one little nugget."

"It is my responsibility to report this matter, Mr. Early, but I will be the soul of discretion. This will not be telegraphed but dispatched by courier as soon as weather permits. Does Colonel Grant know of this nugget or was there any discussion pertaining to gold with him in your presence at any time?"

"No, sir, not to my knowledge."

"Very well. I will keep this safe for you while you are in the guardhouse and return it to you if you are freed."

Custer sat down. "I want to be fair with you in regard to the Mueller incident - but my hands are tied here. I can, however, intervene for your comfort and will do so. You will not be held in irons at any time because you are not a threat to this command."

"I don't want you in the general jail population while you are at the guardhouse and I'll see that your cell door is left open at all times so you can have heat and light from the guard room. You may close it when you sleep if you wish, and it will remain unlocked, but you can't step out into the guard room. I'll make some other routine instructions."

Custer sat at his desk and made lengthy notes of his directions. "You're essentially under house arrest as an officer would be. It's just that your quarters are not suitable for that usual arrangement. Any questions or comments, Early?"

"Thank you, sir. You're very generous and I'm grateful. Just one thing, some of the prisoners don't have winter coats or foot gear yet and there don't seem to be bedsacks in the solitary cells. Any chance for those?"

"I'll see to it. You have to realize that line troops aren't going to like you very much while you're waiting trial. This command is close - like a big family - I'm proud of that. Just tough it out. I personally trust you, Mr. Early - don't let me down."

"Count on it, sir. Thanks."

Custer opened his study door and addressed the guards, handing them his signed notes. "Please give these instructions to the O.D. when you return. This man will no longer need to be in irons."

THIRTY THREE

EARLY LAID A BOOK down on the table that General Custer had ordered to be furnished to his cell. It would soon be too dark to read now. He could hear the sounds of the garrison assembling on the parade ground for retreat and roll call.

He drank the last swallow of coffee, cold now in the tin cup. He briefly thought of asking a guard for hot coffee, a privilege extended to him by Custer, but decided to lie on his bunk instead.

His cell was warmer now. Heat from the fireplace made his space almost as warm as the main guardroom. Deep snow, drifted against the building, helped to keep the heat in and the cold out. By now, he was used to the constant noise from the duty troops.

The guards had come to accept his presence but no one was friendly and he often heard mean comments about his favored treatment ordered by the general. Resentment was still sometimes shown in a shove or a guard's angry impatience with his response to some insolent demand. His treatment was as good as he could expect. They hated his guts but their discipline forced them to obey the general.

Early woke up hours later to the sounds of a large group of men coming into the guardroom, stomping snow off their boots and talking loudly. He could hear even more men in the sally port outside the guardroom door. Walking to his open cell door, he saw Captain Tom Custer, the general's brother, leading a tall, young indian into custody who was wearing manacles.

The indian was wrapped in a blanket and looked frozen. All their faces, both troops and prisoner, were weather burned from the stinging needles of snow driven by the sharp, always blowing, prairie wind.

From conversation between Captain Custer and the guards, Early learned the indian was a Sioux, Rain-in-the-face. He was arrested for killing two white civilians while they were on the Yellowstone expedition last summer.

The troops had picked up the alleged murderer on the Standing Rock reservation where Rain-in-the-face had been bragging about making the kills. Captain Custer and all the troopers seemed very pleased with bringing this killer to justice.

Jim watched as the surly civilian grain thief was brought from his cell and, over his loud and never ending protests, was shackled to the indian with leg irons. The two of them were led hobbling back to the corner cell farthest from the fireplace. Jim heard the cell door slam shut and the clank as it was barred. After much exuberant back-slapping, Captain Custer and his horse troop withdrew.

"Shut up in there. We just got you a squaw humper for a bunky. You two can keep warm cuddling up together." The guard laughed harshly as he pounded on their cell door. The civilian's muffled reply was a raw reference to the guard's ancestry.

Hundreds of reservation indians from Standing Rock rode into Fort Lincoln the next morning as prisoner exercise and guard mount were being conducted. Jim thought it fortunate that the arrival of the Sioux was at a time when a goodly amount of the 7th was already armed and mounted on the parade ground in the center of camp.

As before, however, the indians had been watched for some time as they approached up the river valley. This time, the post was ready. Mounted troopers began riding single file, nose to tail, out of every stable, forming up into their separate troops.

Riding smartly in companies, each with mounts of a different color, the 7th Cavalry wheeled onto the field joining the guards and facing the arriving Sioux. Guidons snapped and bugles blared in an impressive array of precision and professionalism.

Wearing their big buffalo winter coats, the soldiers formed an awesome field force that the indians wouldn't dare tempt to battle. "Present arms" was called and there they were, 600 troops on horse, loaded rifles in their hands, ready for anything.

The Sioux rode slowly onto the field in no formation or order.

They looked not competent to provoke, and not interested in provoking this magnificent army. They formed long wavy lines sitting side by side facing the troops. Wrapped in a wild array of blankets, they made a colorful contrast to the white snow and to the dark uniformity of the troops. General Custer rode out to parley with the chief.

"A'right, show's over. Everyone back inside. You men wanta die o' pneumonia?" The Sergeant and Corporal of the Guard, and the other guards herded the prisoners back into the sally port and then into their locked and guarded areas. The guards had been interested enough in the unfolding drama that they had delayed ending the prisoner exercise so they, themselves, could watch as long as possible.

An hour later, word came to escort Rain-in-the-face to General Custer's quarters. The guards removed the leg iron from the white citizen and clamped it around the warrior's other ankle. They also handcuffed him and threw an army coat over his shoulders.

The Sgt. of the Guard asked the messenger from headquarters, "What's goin' on?"

"Don't know. All Ah know is the ginr'l's office is full o' warhoops waitin' to see this un and tryin' ta bargain fer his release."

"Surely, the ginr'l won't turn him loose."

"A'course not. Ya think old Curley'd turn this murderin' dog out? Ah don' think so. Specially since Cap'n Tom and his boys 'most froze ta death ridin' ta the res and back ta git 'im. Naah, this un'll hafta love solitary 'afore he's through."

Several hours later the guard detail brought Rain-in-the-face back, walking slowly through the snow, keeping pace with the indian's shuffle in his leg irons.

The returning detail talked animatedly for hours about the exciting events that made this day stand out from the usually boring sameness of frontier camp life in the winter.

A sentry coming off post reported the big Sioux party had ridden out of camp before dark and headed downriver again.

Weeks later in the black of night, a gang of civilians from Bismarck, friends of the grain thief, peeled siding boards off the outside of the cell of the citizen and his Sioux fellow prisoner. There was so much card game noise and merriment in the guardroom and with the cell door closed, the break-in went unnoticed. The solitary cells were along the back side of the building which was not often observed during the night.

One wall plank in the corner by the floor had warped enough to loosen the nails. The inmates peeled it back with their hands. Their friends on the outside passed them a carpenter's iron bar which helped them get several planks partially off.

In half an hour, the prisoners had a hole to crawl out. Even moving as carefully as they could, the iron anklets bit into their flesh cruelly as they pulled against each other. Rain-in-the-face wrapped the army blankets around himself.

The blacksmith from across the river clipped the chain between the leg cuffs and the civilians sneaked back to their boat hidden by the river. Rain-in-the-face started on a long, cold trek to join Sitting Bull and his hostile camp. It was snowing and all the tracks were filled in by daylight.

"Look-a-here," the guard sucked in his breath as he opened the cell door the next morning to give the imprisoned pair their breakfast. As the guards gathered at the now vacant cell, one trooper recalled being Rain-in-the-face's guard at his officer's inquiry.

"I brung this redskin inta Jack's office. He looked like one mean sunabich when he was standin' proud 'afore 'em officers. He confessed ta bashin' in Mr. Baliran's head in the Yellowstone with his war axe while he was still alive. He said he killed vet surgeon Honsinger with his rifle shot, but Ah guess he give him a couple love taps anyhoo. He was real mad 'cause they did'n haf good scalps. One was bald and t'other had his hair cut real short."

"Oh, one more thing, he said somethin' in indian and the interpiter dint repeat it in english til the ginr'l made him do it."

"What?" another guard asked.

"The interpiter turned ta Cap'n Tom and told him this big buck said he'd git the Cap'n some day and cut out his heart and eat it. He meant it, too, ya could tell. Mean sunabich. I'd hate ta have him on my trail and now he's loose."

The Corporal of the Guard looked pale, Jim thought. This killer escaping on his watch was his responsibility and he'd be court-martialed for it. Early turned to his table to finish his breakfast.

"Keep that door shut 'til we get the wall fixed or everyone'll freeze in here," the O.D. said. "I'll get the post carpenter over ta start repairs. Make your report, Corporal, the General will wanta talk to ya."

"Want us ta put out a detail ta look fer tracks, sir?"

"Yes, Sgt., on horseback, but I'm afraid the snow has covered their tracks pretty good. Don't worry about the citizen, he won't ever steal grain again. Just try for the indian and report back."

Hours later, the detail gave up and Jim heard the sergeant report the failure of their reconnaissance to the new Sgt. of the Guard at the desk in the guardroom.

THIRTY FOUR

ON THE NIGHT OF February 8, General Custer's big, splendid house caught on fire. The roof of the house blew off with an explosion. The sentinel at the guardhouse fired his rifle as an alarm and all troops including the prisoners were turned out to help.

When Jim arrived, the general was in a long nightdress with his vest buttoned over it, standing on the landing at the top of the grand staircase, calmly directing the removal of possessions. He was covered with chunks of plaster and plaster dust. The entire upper story was in flames, there was no way to save the house.

Jim was glad to see that Josiah was among the men feverishly working to beat the fire to the general's finery. He saw Mrs. Custer in her nightdress take Agnes, one of her housemaids wrapped in a blanket, across the snow to Captain Custer's house next door. The night air was below zero but there was no wind so there wasn't much danger of the fire spreading across officer's row.

In half an hour, all that was left of General Custer's quarters was smoldering, glowing coals and a small pile of household belongings that the men had carried to the parade ground.

Custer addressed the troops. "Thanks, men. Wasn't much we could do to save it. We'll rebuild it ourselves on this foundation. We'll start tomorrow."

"How did the fire start, sir?" Early was standing near the general.

"Not sure, Early, but we've had problems with the chimney to an upstairs fireplace. All the fires were banked up tonight, so a hot chimney could have been the cause - not really sure."

"Sorry, sir. Looks like almost a total loss."

"We'll just start over. I'll try to convince Mrs. Custer that it will

157

be fun to 'make do' until spring when we can bring in new clothes and furniture on the train," he smiled wryly. Moving close to Jim, the general slipped something into his hand. It was the nugget. Early looked surprised.

"Well, I was keeping it safe for you. Wouldn't do to lose it while it was in my possession," the general smiled. "Actually, it was in my purse which was in this vest along with my gold watch. Please don't tell anyone about the gold, Mr. Early, but you'd better take care of it yourself now."

"Not a word to anyone, General."

"By the way, there'll be no inquiry tomorrow. I'll set a new date which will be soon. Mueller is alright physically now. We'll move him from the hospital to the other side of the guardhouse tomorrow."

Early nodded as Custer walked away. He turned to see Josiah standing a little apart in the dark. "You alright, Josiah?"

"Yes, sir, Jim. I'm fine. My English has improved, what do you think?"

Early's wide grin answered him. "Remarkable, Josiah, can you read?"

"Some, Jim, thanks to you and the general. We're getting there," Josiah chuckled. "Mary, the cook, say I'm de mos' uppity niggah she hav evah seen." Jim laughed at the imitation of Mary's accent which was almost the same as Josiah's had been not too long ago.

Josiah's face went grave and anxious. "How you doin' in jail? Mueller had it comin', I know that."

"If he had just not pushed me into a life or death situation, we'd both be free as a bird. I acted in self defense within the limits of the law. I think I'll get out soon. I don't know what will happen to Mueller."

"I'm taking good care of Buck, Jim. She'll be glad to see you back I'm sure. Never did ride her, though, too much snow. I hope your court turns out right and you can go back to your cabin."

"Me, too, Josiah. Have to go. Thanks for watching Buck." Jim fell in with the prisoner detail as they marched away to the guardhouse.

THIRTY FIVE

ON THE SECOND EVENING after the fire, the general and Mrs. Custer moved into the other half of Tom Custer's house. Their remaining personal possessions were now scattered among the standard furnishings of a cavalry officer's quarters. The total effect was pleasing enough and comfortable.

A doorway had been cut through the wall between their separate quarters. Now, this close family could better mingle together during the bitter sub-zero weather without having to go outside from door to door.

The general and Mrs. Custer entertained immediately and Mary and Josiah prepared and served a sumptuous supper for the post officers and their wives. The entire house was ablaze with lights and every fireplace was roaring hospitably.

The military band played a concert beginning with "Home Sweet Home" to the absolute delight of General Custer's wife Elizabeth, whom the general affectionately called Libby. They made the most of their reduced living space which was, after all, more palatial than many quarters they had shared on the frontier. All the officer's wives, led by Libby Custer, spent two days after the fire refurnishing the wardrobes and personal needs of Mrs. Custer's housemaids. Clothing was culled from their own closets, or sewed up from materials on hand or purchased in Bismarck. The girls had lost everything in the fire, even their purses, so the general made sure they had pocket money again.

General Custer made sure Josiah and Mary were refurnished with ample clothing and personal gear. Josiah was assigned to sleep on a couch in the general's study.

General Custer prepared plans for his new home to be built on the site of the grand house he had just lost. He and his wife decided on some alterations to the standard military plan of the first house, including a huge bay window in the center of the south wall of the parlor, a private dressing room off the master bedroom, and a long billiard room on the second floor.

Re-arrangement and enlarging of the main floor rooms occupied all the space of the new construction without allowing for a kitchen. Therefore, a large kitchen addition was planned on the back of the new house. The front veranda would be wider and also extended along the north side in the manner of southern plantation mansions. The new house would be grander.

There were plenty of materials left over from the summer construction. Fort Lincoln boasted its own sawmill for cutting and planing fill-in pine boards and planks. The post carpenter could run crews of troopers rebuilding the commanding officer's housing and keeping the men occupied through the dreary winter.

General Custer instituted mail service to and from St. Paul Regimental Headquarters commanded by General Sturgis. A covered army wagon box mounted on bobsled rails, pulled by four sturdy mules, was driven by a loyal, reliable cavalry sergeant. The service made a round trip of 500 miles in about two weeks running along the telegraph line. This courier made possible the exchange of military orders, dispatch pouches, and the delivery of personal mail on a regular basis for the rest of the winter.

Although the teamster job was full of hardships, there was never a shortage of heroic sergeants contesting for the honor of making the next trip. Sometimes the telegraph was also usable but it was unreliable because lines were frequently down from ice and snow loads, and, telegrams afforded no privacy for sensitive messages.

Relying on the wagon courier service, Custer issued several sealed dispatches to General Sheridan in Chicago during the winter and received secret replies the same way.

In the second week after his house burned down, Custer conducted Jim Early's officers inquiry and Sgt. Mueller's courts martial separately in his new parlor in his temporary home.

With testimony from the 7th Cavalry witnesses and pertinent

remarks from Lt. Colonel Grant and General Custer, the officers found Early innocent of any wrongdoing and ordered his release for the good of the service with apologies. Early regained favor with most troopers when they realized he had been unjustly held for so long.

Unanimously, the officers found Mueller guilty of several charges, stripped him of his stripes, and ordered him confined to a solitary cell to be shipped to Federal prison on the first available transportation. With his right arm stumped above the wrist, Mueller was pale and despondent in the court and then in black depression during his confinement in the Fort Lincoln guardhouse. He raved madly and cursed his former mates who were now his captors.

In April, Custer received a wire from Congressman Robert Elliott of South Carolina requesting any information he might be able to furnish about any suitable colored candidate who could be endorsed for admission to West Point. Custer was flattered at this apparent recognition, both political and military.

He had long cherished the thought that he might some day be able to parlay his own brilliant army career into the highest office of the land as U.S. Grant had. He well knew there were political president makers who held the same idea. He was anxious to do favors for the country's leaders.

Custer called Fred Grant in for conference, showing Grant the wire he had just received. "What about Pvt. Briggs, Colonel?" Custer asked point blank. "He's clean, serious about his duties, and has no bad habits; and it's unbelievable how quickly he has learned to read and how well he speaks now."

Grant was stunned and didn't know what to say. "I've noticed his speech, sir. It's amazing. I would have to say he endured our ordeal last summer as well as anyone, and with a serious wound, too." Grant paused. "May I say, however, I am not particularly a proponent of darkies in the military. Black officers are unheard of. Even the Union Army in the war officered colored troops with white officers. This kind of idea is the product of the reconstruction carpetbaggers. Are you for it?" He couldn't believe it.

"Wasn't there a black cadet in your class at the Point? Was it Smith?"

"Yes, sir, but he had a rough ride for four years and was finally found deficient in philosophy when our class graduated."

"So, Smith didn't graduate?"

"No, sir."

"Was he hazed as a plebe?"

"For four years by everyone. He was called every name in the book. Well, you can imagine. One moke in a white military school, especially a school with the proud tradition of the Point. He was the object of constant ridicule. No, that would not be an enviable position to be in. So far, there has yet to be a black officer in this army."

Custer fiddled with his mustache. "I'm going to ask him if he wants to go. If he does, I'll recommend him. He's intelligent and has shown good character and ability. I want you to stand with me and ultimately to stand by Briggs. As my aide, you can help me prepare him if he's accepted at West Point."

"Yes, sir, if that's your decision."

Custer called Josiah into the study and closed the door. "At ease, Briggs." He showed his orderly the telegram. "Do you understand the message?"

"Of course, sir."

"I want to submit your name to the Congressman as a candidate. How would you feel about that?"

"I wouldn't be qualified, sir."

"Colonel Grant and I would work on you night and day until you depart, if you are accepted. I can also get Early in on this. Let me say, however, that one colored cadet among hundreds of whites - where no black has ever graduated - might be in a very hostile situation. I have no doubt you would do well, Briggs, if you could take the hazing."

"I'm tough, sir. I'm not scared to try."

"Very well Briggs, I'll wire the Congressman today. That's all."

Two weeks later, General Custer received a sealed dispatch from Congressman Elliott with signed approval by General Sheridan in

Chicago and a terse note from the general to make sure this was a candidate who would reflect honor upon the 7th Cavalry.

As an afterthought on the note, he also said "I hope you know what you are doing here, my friend. Orders will follow." Custer couldn't wait to tell Josiah. Josiah was elated and went to share his news with Early that evening after supper.

In the same dispatch case, Custer received information from General Sheridan that he should begin preparing the 7th for a summer campaign to the Black Hills.

```
TO WIT:
ORDERS WILL FOLLOW FOR AN OFFICIAL
MISSION TO THE BLACK HILLS TO LOCATE
A POSSIBLE SITE FOR STRATEGIC MILITARY
POST AND TO MAP AND DESCRIBE THIS AREA.

Do not reveal that a major part of your
job is to make a first-hand survey of
the likelihood of any major amounts
of gold that might be obtained there.
I want you to follow up on your scout
lead. Be sure he accompanies you to
point out the location. Let me stress,
General, that gold is a secret agenda
known only to you and me at this point.
You may take a civilian miner or two
along as might be publicly expected.
Do not give them time or access to
likely situations, but allow them only
minimal access to unlikely locations.
Their findings may be released upon your
return if, in your judgement, their
conclusions are not inflammatory to the
white population or to the indians. I
rely on your judgement here, General.
This is to be billed as a scientific
undertaking for the U.S. Government and
we need to get word to the indians that
this is not an attempt to renege on the
treaty and take over the Black Hills.
```

Conduct your gold search secretly with
one or two individuals you can trust
completely, perhaps your scout, and who
are sworn to absolute secrecy in the
matter. Report your findings to me in
sealed dispatch when you return to Fort
Abraham Lincoln.

URGENT.

    SIGNED LT. GENERAL PHILIP H. SHERIDAN
                              U.S. ARMY.

THIRTY SIX

SUNSHINE AND WARM BREEZES melted the snow almost every day as spring approached. The drifts were subsiding and bare, muddy spots appeared between the dirty, porous drifts that had been blown up by the wind. Green grass shoots in the bare spots gave promise that winter was finally over.

Work on General Custer's house moved much more quickly in the balmy weather than it had in the icy gales. In fact, the structure had been closed in and men were working inside. Other crews were working on the veranda outside and digging foundations for the big kitchen and the dressing room.

Custer moved knowingly among his troops, encouraging them and showing them what he wanted and how he wanted it. The general did not allow for variation between the specification and the completed job, and the men knew it.

"Mr. Early, when you and your helper are through trimming out this doorway between the parlor and the dining room, would you help the post carpenter with the butternut balustrade that I want running up the staircase to the second floor?"

"Yes, sir, we'll be done here today."

"This looks very nice."

"Yes, sir, there's enough of this wide oak trim left over from the first construction that we can match grain and color on all the doorways."

"Will someone be working on these fireplace fronts now?"

"Yes, sir, that's next in this room. They'll start on that tomorrow and John here can help with that. How big a job will the stair railing be?"

"Done right, it will probably take you and the carpenter the rest of the week in his shop with his tools. Butternut will turn out beautiful, but it's hard to work. He's got a piece left over like they used the first time."

"I'll check in with him in the morning, sir."

"When will your winter hitch be up, Early?"

"Next month, sir."

"Will you sign on for summer?"

"Don't think so, General; I have some personal things to tend to."

"Come to my office next Monday at ten hundred hours, will you, Early? I'd like to discuss this with you."

"Yes, sir. By the way, how's Pvt. Briggs doing? Haven't seen him for a while. He doesn't work on the house."

"I haven't had as much time to spend with him as I'd like - but Col. Grant has given him study assignments and then tested him - Colonel says he soaks it up."

"He feels free for the first time in his life, sir. I hope this appointment doesn't turn out to be a big disappointment for him. He really believes in it and is very grateful to you."

"Early, would you teach him to shoot and to ride? After noon Monday, I can relieve you of all other duties until your hitch is up - if you will teach Briggs all you can - especially everyday social conduct and practical things."

"Can he stay in my cabin? He'll need a Springfield and a Colt and a horse to use. We don't have much time left."

"Have him draw a rifle and a pistol from Sgt. Thompson and I will clear it with Sgt. Towers for him to get the cull four-year old gelding that is a mate to your mare. Yes, he's yours, Early. We want him to be a credit to this command when he goes to Washington."

"He'll do his best, sir. Thank you!"

"I hope you realize I'm losing the best striker I ever saw," Custer said with a slight smile and a twinkle in his eye. "You two better not fail me." Custer went out through the open front door.

Josiah moved his gear to Jim's cabin after chow that evening. He was very excited about the West Point opportunity. They stopped at the guardhouse and asked the duty Corporal to have a fatigue detail deliver a load of hay the next day to the cabin for bedding and to cover the dirt floor.

For the first night, they moved the old hay around and made do. They talked for hours about what Josiah would need to know that he could learn from Early. Jim was comfortable again in his cabin. This was the most private place to live that he'd had since he left home to go to war, and the most private that Josiah had ever had.

The next morning, they drew all the gear Josiah would need and saddled their mounts. Jim figured it was good that Josiah had drawn a gelding to learn to ride on. A mare would be too unpredictable and flighty and a stallion would be too much for a new rider.

"What do you call this horse, Sgt.?" Early asked Towers.

"Nothin' special. Call it what ya want. No one has fooled with this hoss all winter."

"Star, Jim, Star." Josiah quickly put in. "I'll call him Star." He was remembering Captain O'Meara's black horse. Josiah put his arm around Star's neck and rubbed his nose. This one was black with a blaze face and four white stockings. Star nosed Josiah's chest.

Jim talked softly to Buck as he got her ready but she was nervous. He had been in the stable a few times lately to hand grain her and curry her down besides her daily care. She was losing her winter hair now and was definitely frisky.

They led their horses outside and Jim swung up on Buck. He didn't have time to settle into the saddle. Buck's hind feet went straight up in the air and she twisted and bucked until, withers heaving, she broke into a jarring trot. Early stayed with her, talking softly and reaching up to rub her neck as she trotted. "Whoa," he said. She pulled up blowing and prancing. Jim reined her around and she walked back to Josiah with her quick stepping gait.

"That's the other reason we called her Buck," Towers sung out from the barn door. Laughing, he disappeared into the shadows.

Josiah mounted Star and was glad the gelding was not high spirited. They rode along the river, picking their way around snow banks and trying to find the rockier, drier going, avoiding the mud as much as possible.

Ice on the river looked rotten like it would break up any day.

A few patches of blue, swift flowing water sparkled out in the channel.

They rode upriver for about an hour and ran their horses back towards the post until they were winded, then walked them to the stable, and rubbed them down before they left them in their stalls.

The two friends rode farther and farther every day, getting used to their mounts and letting the horses get used to them. Josiah had never ridden a horse before, just a mule some, so their daily rides were absolutely thrilling to him. He felt freedom he had never known. Early was having a good time, too. Buck settled down and horse and rider became like one again.

"Tomorrow, we'll get you on some target practice, Josiah, up above the bluffs," Jim gestured above the camp. "We'll start you with the rifle."

As the days and weeks passed, Josiah's skills improved. He was a quick learner, eager to make the most of this chance to learn from Jim and to please his friend with good results. They moved their horses to the cabin. They talked to Two Strike and his wife and played with the little boys.

In the evenings by the fire in the cabin, Jim set up mathematical problems verbally and Josiah worked out the answers mentally. On clear nights, Jim taught him practical navigation techniques by the stars. Astronomy it wasn't, but he shouldn't be overwhelmed when faced with understanding the subject as taught by a professor.

Every day Josiah read aloud to Jim in the morning sunlight, reading and rereading everything they could lay their hands on. Jim talked about military strategy as he understood it and his experiences in the war, both good and bad. He talked to him about practical matters of command and relationships with subordinates.

Early checked on Josiah's knowledge of the material that Grant had given him in the first days of his preparation. Jim amplified on that information as he could.

"Remember, and think about, everything you heard from General Custer and Colonel Grant, and everything you saw and heard in the big house, until it's part of you, Josiah. They both graduated from West Point so they've learned first hand what will be expected of you at the Point."

"Captain O'Meara and I officered during the war and came to the rank of Captain in the field. All any of us can do for you is prepare you as much as we can for that university level education. It's up to you when you get there."

"Let's saddle up," Jim said. Another long day of work lay ahead.

THIRTY SEVEN

MONDAY MORNING OF THE week after Jim finished working on Custer's house, he reported to the general's office at 10:00 sharp. As Custer closed the door to the hall, Jim noticed a military map on the wall that roughly showed features of the territory. Fort Abraham Lincoln and Bismarck, the Northern Pacific Railroad and the Missouri River were precisely located near the east edge of the map. The Black Hills were shown as a dark mass in the lower left quadrant. Some rivers were crudely traced and named but not much else. French Creek - ah, French Creek, not Frenchman's Creek as he had remembered it - was shown flowing out of the east side of the Hills. The Cheyenne and the Belle Fourche Rivers looked like forks of the same river.

"Mr. Early, confidentially, I have orders to take the entire regiment to the Black Hills this summer on an exploratory expedition. I have scouts, but you are the only one who's been there," Custer waved his hand in the direction of the map.

"I expect this to take about sixty days, probably July and August. We'll field a large force in case we have indian trouble. There are reports this spring about Crazy Horse raiding and killing whites north of Fort Laramie, keeping the white miners out of the Black Hills from the southwest. We've also had reports from all over the territory of other Sioux raids. They're leaving the reservations in large numbers."

"Nevertheless, this is not to be a punitive expedition nor an attempt to conquer or take back treaty lands. We hope to fill in some of the blank areas on this map with some details and hope to find a good site for a military fort near the Hills. I would very much like to have you with me as my head scout - can we strike a deal?"

"Sir, no disrespect to you, but don't forget that I spent about half of my winter hitch in the guardhouse here. You have more than made up to me for that, but it was an unpleasant experience and I feel like moving on. Also, I wouldn't like to be head scout of a large military expedition, and I don't want to be tied up for another six months."

"Have you lost your stomach for indian engagements? I wouldn't blame you if you had."

"Hardly."

"Well, then ... would you go on the expedition with us as a guide paid out of my post operating budget? On that basis, you wouldn't have to sign for a scout hitch."

"Can you pay me for my winter enlistment when it's up?" "Yes, same way. Whatever you have coming, I'll pay you. Regular pay call won't come through until we're on the road to the Hills, but we'll handle yours now."

"Is the gold involved?"

"I have told you our official purposes. If indians interfere with our movement, we'll fight. My 7th, 1000 men strong under my command, can whip every indian on this continent, all at the same time."

"... and the gold?"

"I'll need you to identify French Creek and where you found your nugget. Could you do that?"

"I think so."

Custer paced, paused, looked directly into Jim's tense face. "You must not reveal any of this discussion until it is released - but, especially, you must never reveal what I'm about to tell you - to anyone - no one at all."

"Yes, sir."

"The general government is interested in the possibility of wealth in the Black Hills. There's a major recession in this country, even railroads are in trouble. People are out of work everywhere. There is great unrest - the easiest way out is further expansion of settlement. New gold would create an instant infusion into the economy and get America moving again." Jim didn't speak for a long time. It was Custer's turn to wait.

"If you catch up my pay promptly at the end of my enlistment and I can live here as I am until the expedition leaves, I'll do it with one further condition."

Custer's body relaxed. "What, sir?"

"As soon as you're satisfied about the gold, I'll be free to ride away."

"By yourself? In the middle of the Sioux nation, with maybe hundreds of Cheyennes around? I don't think it would be wise. Why would you want to do that?"

"Personal reasons, sir. It's that or I can't go along. I'll leave the Hills across the badlands back to Yankton. The indians will be watching you. They won't see me and I will do nothing to incite them, I swear."

"Very well, Early - I want you as a guide - you give me no choice. Whatever you want to do."

"At what pay, sir?"

"I'll give you $100 a month out of my budget for two months, plus horse allowance when you leave the command."

"Deal, sir." They shook hands. Both men had got what they wanted and were satisfied.

THIRTY EIGHT

ON THE TOP OF the bluffs above the Missouri River, Josiah was still having some trouble with his target practice.

"Maybe you're good enough to hit an indian, Josiah, but you're not sharp. Here's an old trick some of the boys in my command found useful in the war." Early held up his right index finger. "What finger is this?"

"Trigger finger."

"Also, it's your pointer finger. Point your pointer finger at that cottonwood. Practice looking away, with your arm at your side, relaxed. Then, point at the tree or any object, time and time again with just your finger." Josiah practiced, but felt foolish.

"Now, take up your rifle and extend your pointer finger ahead of the trigger guard along the breech. Your middle finger will fall naturally inside the trigger guard and will now be your trigger finger. Try it and hit that cottonwood. Just look at the tree, point at it with your finger, and squeeze. Don't pay any attention to the sights."

Josiah hit the tree.

"Good. Practice coming up quick, point and shoot. Here, use my Winchester and empty it out."

Josiah missed the tree the first two shots.

"Settle down, don't breathe when you shoot."

Josiah concentrated and hit the tree thirteen times in quick succession.

"How does that feel, Josiah?"

"Feels good, Jim, feels good. Where'd you learn that?"

"It was an idea shown to us by an old squirrel hunter from Tennessee who certainly didn't need any marksmanship crutches himself. He said his grandpappy taught him to hunt that way when he was a kid."

"It gives you the feeling you need and you're a natural. When your eye and your rifle focus together most of the time, you can go back to using your pointer finger for a trigger finger, if you want to. Whatever is most comfortable."

Jim loaded the carbine again, handed it to the shooter, and stood behind Josiah. Ten shots, ten hits followed. "Alright, that's all of my ammo I can spare. Use your Springfield and keep practicing. You're already as good as any of Custer's troopers. They don't 'waste' ammo practicing but since the general says that you can burn 'em up, do it."

"Jim, your carbine is really nice to shoot. I like it better than the Springfield."

"So do I, but that Springfield's a killer for accuracy when you're using the sights. General Custer's a fine marksman and he's advising the military commanders to stick with it. They all agree - big bullet, flat shooter over long distances, fine sights ... but, they're giving up the repeater advantage in battle situations."

"I think the availability of fifteen shots when you're in a tight spot, gut to gut, outweighs the accuracy thing. As an officer, you can use whatever you want to. If you want a repeater, you may have to buy your own and your own ammo. For now, get used to the single shot."

Josiah practiced until his arm got sore and he was pulling his shots.

"That's enough for today. Tomorrow, we'll give your arm a rest."

As they rode off the high plateau towards the bluffs, they heard a popping, droning noise that kept getting louder as they approached camp. When they reached the bluffs, they were startled by loud reports from the river, almost like explosions. The ice on the river was breaking up and the crashing sounds could be heard a long way - at the top of the bluff, the roar was almost deafening.

Early and Josiah dismounted to watch. Troopers, officers, and officer's wives were straggling up the hill to see from the bluffs near the infantry post on top. Infantry soldiers poured out and joined the cavalry ranks. What a huge collection of blue uniforms and ladies, Early thought. A picnic atmosphere prevailed and there was much shouting in wonder and awe.

The river was out of its banks from the spring melt and was throwing up huge blocks of ice along the shores. The low land across the river was flooded by the swift-flowing water and the level was rising.

The Whiskey Point people had gathered on a slight rise in their area. Although, the shacks on the slight elevation were still standing, many of the mean huts below them were collapsing in the current and washing away. They were surrounded by water, even cut off from Bismarck by the raging torrent.

A loud, collective cry went up from the military group. A man, and then a woman, climbed into the only small boat they seemed to have over there, and shoved off from the threatened little island. The small boat whirled on the mad river, out of control, and capsized before it had gone a hundred yards. The two from the boat were not seen again. The overturned boat bobbed along and was soon out of sight.

Though they considered Whiskey Point and its citizens to be buzzards who preyed upon the soldier's needs for entertainment, the Fort Lincoln officers sympathized with their plight this day.

Jim and Josiah rode down the hill to their camp. The officer's wives slowly walked down as a group, no longer able to bear watching the fate of those across the river.

As the pair was unsaddling behind the cabin, Two Strike's squaw came around the corner of the building with arms outstretched in front of her. She was smiling from ear to ear, carrying a complete set of new buckskins and a new pair of buffalo hide moccasins. "Wife found old moccasins in cabin when you were gone, Early," Two Strike said as he followed her. "She make you new ones."

Early admired the buckskins. She had decorated them with fringe like his old ones but she had also done a lot of colorful quill work in the Indian way. She shyly walked up, then hugged him as he stood holding the clothes. "Brother," she said, looked him in the eyes, and hurried back to her lodge. Early murmured thanks to Two

Strike, asked him to be sure she understood how grateful he was, and the two talked a few minutes before they parted.

"They're good people, Josiah."

Josiah grinned. "I can see they think the world of you, as I do, and as the general does. That seems to happen to you a lot. S'pose there's a reason?"

Early didn't answer. He went into the cabin to change into his new, comfortable trail clothes.

During the afternoon, the river went down enough for the survivors at Whiskey Point to be safe. Those who still had buildings started to clean up and to get ready for business. The spring flood, high water danger was over for another year.

The river ferry was battered but still floating and still tied to the dock on the Bismarck side of the river. Heavy hawsers, well tied to stanchions on the dock, had saved the old river boat. It was running again a couple days later as the mud in Whiskey Point, and on toward Bismarck, started to dry and the ice chunks melted.

Troopers in dress uniforms took Mueller to the first train to leave for the Twin Cities. The light of madness was in his eyes as he shuffled against his leg irons and cursed his guards. An armed escort would accompany him to prison.

THIRTY NINE

SNOW SPRAYED FROM THE base of the limestone rim and cascaded down the mountainside high in the western Black Hills. The great grizzly, bursting through the snow drift covering the entrance of his winter den, stood blinking in the bright, early spring sun. A slight breeze carried the faint smell of thawing, rotting meat. He was drowsy and not hungry.

He moved around the narrow ledge in front of his cave, sniffing and yawning with muted noises. He lay on his belly in the sun for a while with his forepaws extended in front of his body and his head resting on them. He got up, stretched, and went back into his den. Winter was starting to release its grip on his world, but the bear was groggy.

The forest was totally still again. Ice and snow covered almost everything except the vertical stretches of grey limestone above the cave. The blinding brightness of sunlight, beating down from a solid blue, cloudless sky, reflected up from the long unmarked white slope below. Dark green needles of pine and spruce branches, appearing almost black from a distance, contrasted starkly with the snow loads piled deeply on them and with icicles sparkling in the sun. No sounds disturbed the stillness.

He was slow and lazy for a week. He didn't stray far from his den during this time, and when he moved, he walked like a huge drunk with uncertain balance. He slept outside in the sun a lot. He gained some strength and agility every day.

Toward the end of his first week out of hibernation, he rolled and slid down the slope below his den and then, with great effort, made his way back up to lay in front of the cave.

Finally, hunger forced him to quit his winter haunt, and to

depart on another six month summer's journey of eating anything he could find, to be ready again for his winter sleep.

His cycle of life continued - eat all summer, sleep all winter. The grizzly had no natural enemies. He was the hunter, never the hunted. He could easily kill anything he could catch, from a field mouse to a sick or weakened elk to a yearling buffalo.

Moving down the mountainside, the great grizzly sought out the winter-killed whitetail deer that had been the source of the teasing scent of rotting meat. The odor had become stronger every day as the sun warmed the countryside. The deer was down by a small spring that poured from the sunny side of the hill and flowed away as a small creek. Along the edges of the stream, tender green grasses were already thick and growing tall.

The bear gorged upon the deer carcass, tearing off big chunks of the meat and swallowing them almost whole with little chewing. Alternately, he grazed the green shoots along the stream.

After he finished with the deer, the big bear moved on, no longer sluggish or unsure, ready for any challenge. One day, he was above the Cheyenne winter camp, which was now bustling with activity, as the indians were coming out of their own winter. The fragrance of human scent reminded him of last summer's successes. The grizzly hesitated but finally moved away from the camp.

In the way of his kind, the grizzly could subsist on grasses and plants in the late spring and summer until berries appeared, but he would never refuse an easy kill for a filling banquet of meat. This bear was oversized, in a large part, because he was more of a meat eater. He was good at finding what he needed to sustain his huge body in these hills where there was usually an abundance of game.

In the Cheyenne camp, Whirlwind Horse met in council with all of the leaders of their band. So far from the marauding white man and with plenty of food stores, good teepees, abundant firewood, and warm skins, the Cheyenne had enjoyed their season of rest.

Now, the men were restless. They had to decide whether to stay by Paha Sapa through yet another winter count, or to move.

Many warriors and their squaws in the village were expecting children. White Calf was big with child and would deliver soon.

Whirlwind Horse was proud and grateful to the Great Spirit for his good fortune. Pretty Voice and the Whirlwind had regained their former closeness and life had been lazy and good through the time of the deep snows.

Tribal leaders argued long and heatedly in council on several occasions without reaching a decision about their camp. Everyone had liked this Paha Sapa place. There was much meat and berries and roots, plenty of fresh water. This spot was protected from the harsh prairie winds and they were safe from the blue soldiers.

The Cheyenne had lost some of the big army horses and some ponies in the bitter cold, but they still had more than enough in their horse herd. They were bony thin now, but they would fatten soon enough. Buffalo were in abundance on the plains and, in early scoutings, the Cheyenne had seen many wobbly buffalo calves in the wild herds.

Yet, many of the people longed to trail for the Powder River country where they could also expect good living; and where they might join up with many other Sioux and Cheyenne and Arapaho bands in favorite summer camps, long established for many generations. It would be good to see and to hunt with old friends.

Paha Sapa should be safe from the wide eyes after their total defeat in the last moon of the heat. This would be a good place to come back for winter camp after a big summer with the other bands. This idea was favored by Whirlwind Horse and many others in the council, but some of the old ones needed the long talk to think of giving up this ideal setting.

Two miles from the Cheyenne village, up a long valley near the crest of the foothills, the great grizzly came upon the thawing body of a cavalry horse that had wandered away in a blizzard and died in the fury of the blinding snow.

Now, the bear would remain in the vicinity for at least a couple of weeks as he relished the carrion he had found. Skulking coyotes abandoned the site when the bear moved in. Crows cawed relentlessly in nearby trees and flew overhead. No vultures showed up. There were so many winter-killed animals in the hills this spring after the severe winter, the vultures were down on other far-flung carcasses. Plenty of food for all the scavengers right now.

One night, as Whirlwind Horse rode in with several big rabbits he had shot, White Calf's time was getting close. He brought Owl Woman to the young mother's side to help her with the baby. The next morning at dawn, a new baby boy was born to the war chief's wife.

White Calf was pale and weak after the exertion of the birth. Owl Woman and Pretty Voice cleaned up the mother and child, then wrapped the boy in soft, new deer skins and placed him in a cradle board. He was big, dark like his father, and well-formed. Whirlwind and his wives decided the new baby should be called White Eagle. They felt this a fitting name for the great warrior they knew he would grow up to be.

FORTY

"MR. EARLY, IS PVT. Briggs ready for his trip to Washington on the Potomac?" Custer asked. Grant was in the general's office with the others. Custer's office was again located in his own quarters, now reconstructed.

"As ready as we can get him in a short time, sir. He is a very good learner. As far as I know, I think he'll do well with the education. I'm not sure about being a colored cadet in an all-white academy like the Point. I don't envy him the experience."

Grant looked away. Custer looked at Josiah without saying anything for a moment. Then, "Briggs, are you ready?"

"Yes, sir. Don't worry about the hostile surroundings. I can take it. I'm ready, sir, and I'll always be grateful to each of you."

"Good, Mr. Briggs - I wish you well. I'm sure you'll graduate from West Point and maybe be the first colored officer in the U.S. Army. I truly hope so."

"Here are your orders. Take the train from Bismarck in three days. Check in your arms and your horse. Pack your personal gear, so you'll be ready to go. As of now, you are relieved of all duties on this post."

"You may continue to stay in Early's quarters until you leave and you can draw your pay here tomorrow. Your records have already been forwarded. May I say, your conduct and service here have been outstanding. You have done a good job, Briggs; keep it up. Early, will you see him off?"

"Yes, sir."

"That's all, gentlemen. Oh, Mr. Early, can you meet with me here this afternoon at 0100?"

"Yes, sir."

Later, Early drew $204 from General Custer for his six months winter hitch less four month's horse allowance. "You know, we'll be forming up next week for the Black Hills. I'm expecting new Springfields to come in for all the troops. I'm excited to see them - an improved model, I understand."

"Good, sir. Thank you. I'll be ready."

Jim and Josiah talked constantly while they waited for Josiah's departure. Before they checked Star back in with Sgt. Towers, they rode across the river and south. No Sioux activity had been observed here since Jim's last ride over this trail. Josiah shot a deer and proudly dressed it. They brought it back to Two Strike's family.

They went over all the training information again and again to be sure Josiah had it down pat. Josiah could read and speak well. He was good on Star and a better shot than many that Jim had seen in the war and since. With the practice of frequent use, Jim thought he could become a crack shot.

One evening, Josiah made a special trip to the back door of the general's house to say goodbye to Mary. She cried, with pride shining through her tears, as they stood in the big, new kitchen.

When Josiah was ready to board the train, Jim pressed $200 in Josiah's hand. When he realized what it was, Josiah's eyes opened wide in astonishment. "No, Jim, I'll get by."

"You'll get by better with a little money. I'm in good shape right now, my friend, and I want you to have this. You'll need money more than I will. Take it." Jim forced Josiah's hand closed over the bills. Tears welled in both their eyes.

"Thanks, Jim. I'll never forget all you've done for me. I hope the next time you see me, I'll be wearing shiny bars."

"You'll get the bars, Josiah. Work hard. Do it for Captain O'Meara, Custer and Grant ... and me ... but you must do it mostly for yourself."

The two men gripped each other's hands and Josiah stepped up on the train car step as the train started to move and the conductor called "B-o-oa-a-rd" for the last time.

FORTY ONE

DRIVEN BY HIGH WINDS, hail the size of a boy's agate marbles, and rain in a downpour battered the tents of the 7th Cavalry and its scouts. They were laid over, waiting to embark on the Black Hills expedition.

The fierce thrust of the storm lasted about half an hour. Soldiers in their low-to-ground A-tents and Indians in their dog tents were all soaking wet when the cloudburst was over.

Early came out of his little tent with his buckskins muddy and wet. Buck was still picket-pinned nearby, shivering and scared. Many horses and mules had been stampeded by the stinging hail. Many soldiers' tents had blown loose from their pegs and lay flattened on the ground.

A thousand 7th cavalry troops, the entire regiment, and a hundred Indian scouts were now straightening up their possessions in the field camp two miles downriver from Fort Lincoln. The temporary camp was in full sight of the barracks and quarters so recently vacated.

Early thought how nice and dry he would be if he were in his cabin. The cursing troopers nearby thought the same about their barracks. When the first raindrops had fallen, everyone had dived for cover in the little tents.

Jim was glad his tent had held - at least the canvas warded off the pelting hail. Behind his tent lay a dead meadowlark, evidently downed by a plummeting hailstone.

In preparing for this expedition, Custer had the luxury of time. He had set up just outside the fort so the command could be sure they had everything they would need before they left their base of supply, and so his troops could start getting used to the hardships of the trail. The general was still awaiting the arrival of the shipment of Springfields and ammunition. Since he was expecting indian trouble, he didn't want to leave without the new ordnance.

Old hands, themselves swearing a few minutes before, now kidded younger troopers about facing up to life in the army. Everyone's disposition improved as blankets and issue clothing flapped in the breeze drying out.

Tents were re-staked, animals brought in, and the regimental band played beautifully beneath a huge rainbow. Brilliant golden cloud strata in the west blended out to pink along the horizon as the sun set.

Lt. Colonel Grant and several other officers had gone south to Fort Rice after the storm on some brief military mission. Grant smiled and nodded at Early as they rode by, chatting among themselves. Early noticed the officers were clean and dry. The wall tents had held against the tempest.

Early grained his horse and went down to the river to wash out his buckskins and clean up. The coolness following the hail and rain was welcome, as it had also been after a long downpour two days before, furnishing relief from the otherwise hundred degree summer heat.

When the Springfields arrived, they were accompanied by new Colt service revolvers like Early's but with standard barrels. The new Springfields were definitely an improved rifle, superior to the older army carbines.

They were, however, .45 caliber and so their ammunition was not interchangeable with the .44 Colt. Troopers had to carry both cartridges. Jim now had unlimited availability of the ammo he would need, he could just draw it from quartermaster.

A few new Winchester carbines came in, too, and were snapped up by the officers. Tom Custer and Fred Grant had seen and admired Early's and decided to carry Winchesters since they had a choice. The general scoffed at their preference and ridiculed their new rifles. Grant and Captain Tom good-naturedly ignored the general's ribbing. Like Early, Grant had used the Spencer repeater in battle and didn't want to have to rely on a single shot when the chips were down.

On this expedition, Custer brought along three Gatling guns which were ten barreled, turned by a simple hand crank, firing ten shots per revolution of the crank. A three inch Rodman howitzer rounded out Custer's invincible armament.

Breaking camp at the crack of dawn, the command headed for the Black Hills. Wagons were surrounded by cavalry and infantry, led by the scouts ahead, forming up four columns.

The giant train was spectacular. Sixty days provisions for this expedition required 110 six-mule army wagons, each carrying five tons of supplies and ammunition for the trip. Right behind the wagons trailed 136 beef cattle and extra horses and mules. Fresh meat would be supplemented by wild game killed along the route. Game hunting would be by authorized shooters only, to include two white frontiersmen who had been hired for hunters.

Indian scouts were commanded by cavalry Lieut. Wallace with Custer's favorite, Bloody Knife, as chief scout. Besides Early, there were two very able white scouts of good reputation, Charlie Reynolds and Louis Agard.

Agard was a squaw man who had lived among the Sioux along the Missouri River for thirty years and spoke the language like a native. No one in the expedition had ever been to the Black Hills except Early.

Since this was called a scientific expedition, there were two scientists along to observe and make measurements and they had special equipment for their use. There were two practical miners, supposedly to check out the feasibility of mining gold in the Hills.

There was a photographer, William Illingsworth, to record what they would see and any events that Custer deemed to be of military or personal importance. Illingsworth had his own enclosed spring wagon for a dark room where he would develop his glass wet plates. He also had a saddle horse. He was important to Custer.

There were six reporters from six newspapers in New York, Chicago, St. Paul, and Bismarck on special assignment to cover for the American public, especially readers in the East, the adventures of the near mythical Custer and this great undertaking.

With so many civilians along, it seemed questionable whether

Custer really expected indian trouble, even though he had prepared carefully for the possibility. Custer's arrogance about the ability of his command would not permit him to think that any amount of plains warriors would dare take them on.

FORTY TWO

IN TWO WEEKS, THE expedition had covered 225 miles as measured by the odometer. With cloudless skies and almost no wind, the heat was stifling and oppressive. Travelling west across the northern prairie of Dakota territory was nearly unbearable; the barren, rocky earth seemed to cover inner fires.

Most of the fair-skinned troopers, including Custer and Early, were soon sunburned with raw, blistered noses and cracked lips. Alkaline dust kicked up by the train added chapping and fiery burning to their discomfort. The fine, powdery dust seeped under their clothing, searing most of their bodies, not just their hands and face.

Forage and water for the mounts and the beef cattle were hard to come by at first. When they found water, it was stagnant and foul. After a few days, the command had passed into more fertile country where the grasses and firewood were plentiful and the water in abundance and good. Increasingly, they moved into preserves populated with antelope and with a few deer. No buffalo were seen, although there were bleached buffalo bones scattered around.

As Early rode up to Custer at the head of the wagon train, summoned by the general, the photographer rode in from a different direction. The two men waited as Custer finished a conversation with the wagonmaster who then rode away. The general wore buckskins with a red silk scarf about his throat. Jim and the general would look a lot alike at a distance.

"Smith's one of the best wagonmasters I've seen," Custer said. "He's good at getting the utmost speed out of the wagons and not slowing up the progress of the train."

"Early, this is William Illingsworth, our photographer. I hear he is also a good hunter. Scouts reported a large herd of antelope ran up that draw to the south as we approached. Would you gentlemen ride over and see if you can knock down some fresh meat for supper? Cut out a couple mules to pack them back."

"Yes, sir," both men responded. An hour later, they were out of sight of the train. The quiet of the open prairie was broken by an occasional meadowlark call or the scream of a hawk on the wing, but there was a constant clatter of hordes of grasshoppers rising in clouds as they rode through the grass.

"Ever see so damn many hoppers, Jim?"

"No, but they're not as bad as the mosquitos were along the river this spring. I was glad to move out of that temporary camp by Lincoln. At least, the hoppers don't bite."

"Hold it, Bill," Jim touched his partner's arm. "There they are."

Both men pulled their rifles. With no further word, the men split up. Illingsworth rode around a small hill beyond the herd and Early moved through some scrub cedar until he was opposite the antelope. He waited until the photographer showed up on the hilltop. Both moved toward their prey on foot, getting into shooting positions. Illingsworth was closer. The antelope froze in alarm, their ears up, poised to run, looking toward the photographer. Three rifle shots popped in quick succession and three animals dropped.

The herd ran toward Early, turning back toward the command as they swept past the scout. Levering four shots from the Winchester, Early dropped four more before the antelope were past. They veered east over the low hill Jim was on and were gone.

"Not bad shootin' for a photographer," Jim teased.

"Noticed you did all right, too."

"Easy shootin'. Poor defenseless things ran right into me. What are you using, a Spencer?"

"Yes, I've had it quite a while. I'm used to it."

"Spencer's good. I've used one a lot, too."

The men loaded their gutted antelope on the mules and rejoining the train, turned the meat over to the cooks. Illingsworth rode to his wagon and handed his horse over to the trooper who had been driving the mules in his absence.

"Bill and I make a pair, General," Early reported in. "Anytime you want to send us on a hunt, we're ready."

"How many did you get?"

"Seven, sir."

"Thanks, Early. My hunters and scouts got a few more this morning. The boys will welcome the change from beef. I want to contest my new Remington against your new Winchester one of these days. Are you up for it?"

"With pleasure, sir."

"My brother, Tom, and Colonel Grant aren't fine game shots, so I haven't had a good comparison yet to see if that Winchester's any good."

"It's good. I'm glad I've got it. Any time, sir."

After crossing into Montana territory, the train turned south toward Wyoming territory, travelling in barren country again, through sagebrush, rocks, cactus, and weeds.

As they passed a prairie dog town, a rattlesnake bit a draft horse by the fetlock just above the hoof. In minutes, the horse was dripping sweat, trembling, and staggering blindly. Jim looked on, horrified, thinking of what Josiah's fate might have been.

Wagonmaster Smith moved in almost immediately and helped the driver unharness. The vet surgeon tied a tourniquet above the bite, cut the fang marks open with a pocket knife to bleed the wounds, and doused the cuts with ammonia. The teamster harnessed a spare horse and the train moved on.

The vet surgeon stayed behind with the sick animal. He led him in to night camp at dark and turned him out with the spare herd. The next time the snake-bit horse was harnessed, he was back to normal.

Very few wild indians had been seen during the trip. Here and there, one or two had been sighted on a distant horizon, and smoke signals had been observed as information was passed in the savage system of communication. None had approached the army. For now, the indians didn't appear to be a threat.

For many miles the command passed through huge rattlesnake-infested prairie dog towns as they travelled south through Wyoming territory. There were no further snake-bite mishaps. Custer pushed the columns hard through long days to get past this inhospitable country. Temperatures reached 107 blistering degrees. Alkali dust raised by their passing bedeviled the expedition.

At last, camping atop a bluff, they were in sight of the Black Hills. Across a badland valley, the Hills loomed up grandly - ten to twelve miles away.

Custer called Early to his tent. "We'll soon be in what I believe will be much better country. Today, rain showers fell on the Hills off and on all afternoon. We didn't even get a cloud for shade."

"Yes, sir, believe me the Black Hills will be heaven after this, cool and nice."

"We're nearing the end of our journey together, Mr. Early. Tomorrow or the next day, we'll be entering the Hills through the west pass described by Reynolds when he came by here fifteen years ago. We have some peaks and rivers named by his, and other, explorations. Captain O'Meara's company last summer, however, was the first white group who ever actually entered into the Black Hills."

"Did you ever hear anything official about why our company was sent in?"

"No. I finally gave up. Some time, I hope to get satisfaction in person from General Sheridan. He won't say a word by post."

"Remember, sir, we were on the other side of the Hills. None of this, so far, is familiar to me. I would say that if our party of survivors had been required to cross this country, without provisions as we were, we wouldn't have made it. I'd suggest you should return to the east and then north, as we did."

"Point taken, Early. This route has been tough."

"I'm anxious to help you locate what you're looking for, General, I've felt useless to you so far."

"Far from useless, Early, you and Illingsworth have been invaluable to this command as meat providers. The hunters I hired have proven far inferior. Of course, I have been fortunate to bag my share of antelope as well - but you have well earned your way on this trip."

Custer wiped the back of his neck with a kerchief. "I only regret that you and I haven't been able to have our shoot-off. Perhaps, we'll still get a chance."

"Perhaps, sir."

The next day, Custer's expedition rode into the outer foothills of the Black Hills. Here, many areas were fertile and had abundant grass. Small stands of pine trees were grouped along the slopes. They encountered several pothole ponds of good water.

Stock and all personnel watered up. The men gratefully washed the alkali dust from their faces, filled their hats with water, and poured it over each other in luxurious cascades.

Custer rode up on his sorrel gelding at a gallop. "Come quickly, Mr. Early, and bring that new gun."

Together, they rode past the main column and, just ahead, Early saw another pothole. This one was set in rolling prairie with brush and trees along the other side. In the middle, was a small flock of ducks. Custer handed Early his glass. "Mud ducks, wouldn't you say?"

"Yes, sir, we called 'em mud hens - no good to eat, they taste muddy."

Dismounting, Custer said, "About a hundred yards, Early. Mud ducks will sit, even when you shoot - they're bobbing on the water and sometimes they dive. Should be a fair competition for our rifles. We can take our time and pick off their heads - let's see who can get the most." The men lay down side by side on a slight rise just above the level of the water.

Custer shot first ... and missed.

"Were you shooting at the one on the left, sir? He ducked on you."

Custer nodded.

Early aimed carefully, holding a fine sight. When he gently pulled the trigger, a duck's head disappeared and the body flailed around, wings flapping. The other ducks swam around undisturbed.

Custer took aim and squeezed one off ... and missed. Early connected again. Two down.

Custer shot ... and missed.

Early wondered if he should pull his shot. Oh, what the hell, it was the general's idea. Third shot, three duck heads in a row.

An agitated sergeant rode up at a wild gallop. "Sir, there's flanker troops t'other side of the brush yonder. Yer shootin' over their heads, sir."

"We better quit, Early. Everyone alright over there, Sergeant?"

"Yes, sir, but anxious."

"Please extend my apologies." Without a glance at Early, the general rode away.

Jim couldn't help the grin. Guess the Winchester would be fine after all.

FORTY THREE

AFTER WHITE CALF'S BABY was born, the tribal council decided they would move the camp for the summer. Together, they decided to travel to the Powder River country where they could hunt with their friends.

Whirlwind Horse suggested they wait a little while before starting so they could replenish their meat stores for the trek. He knew there were hard stretches of country to cross before they would get into Red Cloud's good hunting country. He didn't want the village to run out of food on the trip. He also wanted new mothers and babies to be ready for the hardships of the trail. All agreed to wait until they were ready.

Buffalo were plentiful along the north and east edges of Paha Sapa extending far out from the hills in large areas where the grass supported the herds. Whirlwind Horse headed up a large hunting party of dog soldiers who were anxious to get moving, and they rode away to the east along the foothills.

One morning after the warriors were gone, White Calf was downstream from the camp sitting in the grass in the warm sun by the swift river. She was softly singing indian lullabies to little White Eagle. A young girl of the village, Morning Flower, came running up out of breath.

"There you are. Magpie wants you to come to your father's lodge and help her. She sent me to find you."

"Watch my son for a few minutes, Morning Flower. I know what she wants and I won't be gone long."

"Well ..."

"Come on, Morning Flower, I'll be right back."

"I'll do it, but don't be gone long."

White Calf laid the baby in the grass near the swift river. Morning Flower sat down on a rock nearby. Her thoughts were far away as White Eagle slept. It was a beautiful day, the rock was warm, a light breeze teased her hair, and the sound of the river was peaceful.

"Whuff." Morning Flower ignored the sound intruding into her thoughts from behind her. As the giant grizzly, on all fours, walked slowly between her and the baby, the young girl was stunned in shock. She watched, disbelieving and afraid, as the bear picked up the small baby in its mouth and swam across the river. The baby's cries were muffled by the sounds of the river.

Morning Flower screamed. She jumped up from the rock and ran screaming toward the village. White Calf met her as she was on the way back to the baby.

"What's wrong?" She grabbed the girl. "What's wrong? Where's my baby?" White Calf looked toward the swift river and saw the bear, disappearing into the brush and trees on the opposite bank, with the small precious bundle swinging from its huge jaws.

White Calf wailed. With tears rolling down her cheeks, she pounded on the young girl's head and shoulders, screaming at her. Morning Flower ran from White Calf's angry blows into the village. Both were crying and screaming.

White Calf slumped to the ground in a heap, wailing the death keen. Morning Flower ran, frightened, to her father's lodge. Pretty Voice came to her sister's side and began wailing, too. There was nothing anyone could do until Whirlwind Horse returned from the hunt.

FORTY FOUR

FLORAL VALLEY, CUSTER NAMED it. As they rode into the Black Hills, the valley was framed by pine wooded hillsides and carpeted with fifty kinds of wildflowers, a cornucopia of colors. This was the "west pass", a valley wide enough to be passable for the huge train. As soon as they were all within the cool shade, Custer called a rest and sent scouts out.

Jim circled north up an easy slope, over the hilltop and into another valley that ran in the same direction as Floral Valley. This one was too narrow and rocky for the command to move through. Crossing the second valley, he rode north to the next ridge and east along the top. He stayed just below the skyline most of the time but crossed over, back and forth, scouting both valleys for an hour or so before turning back to camp.

This country was paradise after the hell of the prairie. The air was clear and fresh, beautifully scented by millions of flowers. Clear, cold water sprung from the mountains and rippled over pebbly stream beds. The ground, though somewhat rocky, was resplendent with pine growth; including many tall, old trees suitable for lumber.

In the small valley, Jim found indian travois trails from years past. By a hillside spring, he found what were probably deer bones scattered around. These were this spring's kill.

Jim's blood pounded in his temples. Around the spring were huge grizzly tracks. Early dismounted, dropped the reins, and let Buck drink from the pure water as he examined the tracks.

The bear had evidently killed the deer or had ravaged the remains of a winter kill. The ground was covered with the overlapping huge tracks indicating the bear had stayed here for some time.

Though he squatted for close inspection, nowhere could he make out a track with a missing claw. The tracks were old now and not clear. The scout thought this must be the bear he wanted because of the size of the tracks. There were no other tracks mixed in, just the one animal.

Early thought it very unlikely that there could be two bears this big in the same range, especially in mountains the size the Black Hills appeared to be. This had to be an old boar grizzly, evidently a loner, who no longer rutted with sow bears in the spring.

Jim collapsed in the grass, thinking of Rose. He could smell her clean skin, and feel the way her body felt against his, that long ago day by French Creek. A drop of spring water splashed on his face was like her tear when he had first held Rose in his arms. It had been a day like this.

Then, the image of her savaged body came to mind and Early rose up with renewed determination to avenge her death. He climbed on Buck and headed to report in.

When Jim got in, Charlie Reynolds had already returned from the south swing reporting it impassable for the train. Neither could any threat be staged from that direction in this area.

Louis Agard and Bloody Knife came back from straight ahead in Floral Valley. They had found a recent campsite of a small Sioux party.

With nothing threatening his command, and with everyone rested and refreshed, Custer put Early, Reynolds and twenty five indian scouts out ahead and moved out down the valley. Two Strike rode beside Jim. All the Santee scouts wore full army uniforms but the Rees were painted and in breech clouts.

Reynolds flanked the scouts on the south and Early and Two Strike ranged out north. Bloody Knife took the indian scout contingent straight down the valley. Custer's command strung out single file back up the valley for two miles.

Illingsworth went ahead of even the front scouts with his dark room wagon, accompanied by Agard and two Rees. They carried the camera equipment to the top of the canyon rim and the photographer shot some striking plates of the train strung out. Illingsworth kept busy recording all the wondrous sights.

As they advanced down the serpentine valley toward the center of the Hills, the pretty sloping hillsides changed to deep canyon walls. They entered the valley of a large, swift stream. Custer thought the bare rock rim looked like castle battlements, so he named this Castle Creek. They camped two nights in this valley.

Days later, Custer's expedition camped in the center of the Hills. Because of the difficulty of moving the entire train through the rough country they found themselves in, and because they had not been bothered by the Sioux, Custer decided to make general camp for a few days and run sorties out south and east to investigate the country.

About ten miles east of the general camp was the tall mountain that was reputed to be the highest elevation in the Black Hills, Harney's Peak. The mountain was named after that grand old soldier, General Harney who had first entered this region when Bloody Knife was a young boy. Harney had observed this prominent point from several directions from the plains outside the Hills.

Named by his expedition, Harney's Peak was one of the few Black Hills locations marked on the maps. Since it was not accurately located nor its height accurately recorded, Custer decided to climb that mountain to its top and rectify those shortcomings.

Custer led a small party of a few cavalry troops as an escort, the three white scouts, several headquarters officers, and the correspondent for the St. Paul Pioneer to record the adventure for his American admirers.

Leaving camp early in the morning, they enjoyed the first half of the journey through park-like meadows. One notable feature was the abundance of berries encountered, especially red raspberries without end. Everyone enjoyed handfuls of the sweet fruit.

Then they picked their way through tangled brush, burned and fallen timber and some mucky, marshy areas. The party ate lunch at the top of what they at first had thought to be Harney's Peak. However, they could see another mountain to the east which was taller still which must be Harney's.

With great enthusiasm, the party climbed the second mountain, only to find yet another that was even taller east of the other two. Custer pressed on to accomplish what he had set out to do.

The cavalry escort remained behind this time and the officers, scouts and the reporter led their horses down a thousand foot decline and then up the side of the true Harney's Peak.

Leaving their horses two hundred feet below the summit, they climbed to the very top with great difficulty. Sometimes they ascended vertical cliffs which required wedging their bodies in crevices and climbing hand over hand like a chimney sweep searching for handholds and footholds. From this vantage point, they could see for miles in the crystal clear air. As Early stood looking southeast, Custer walked up to his side. In low tones, Early confided, "General, I recognize the country south of us. We can ride from camp directly to French Creek through this series of valleys very easily." He indicated the French Creek valley to Custer.

Custer hid his excitement from the others. "Let's take Bloody Knife and your friend, Two Strike, and go hunting tomorrow," Custer said quietly.

"Ready when you are, General. Do you want to take your miners along?"

"No."

"Very well, sir."

After making some observations for mapping purposes, they started their return to camp. Because of the extra mountain ascents, they were very late starting back.

At dark, the officer's party was well ahead of the escort troops so they stopped and waited for them to catch up. The general ordered all hands to stay closed up. Riding in moonlight, they arrived at base camp after midnight.

FORTY FIVE

A FEW MINUTES AFTER reveille next morning, Custer sent word for Early to join him at the horse corral to go on a hunt. Jim had Buck saddled and ready when the general rode up on his sorrel gelding, Vic. Custer was trailing four greyhounds of his own as was customary for him.

As they started east, Bloody Knife and Two Strike joined them. Leading three mules, they rode along behind the two buckskin clad men. Custer gave instructions that they would not hunt until they were returning to camp.

Riding at a canter until they were out of sight of the camp, they rode southeast down a pleasant valley. Buck and Vic set the stiff pace easily. They were both frisky in the crisp mountain air. The indian scouts followed more slowly on their ponies and when there was about a half mile spacing, Custer slowed Vic to a fast-stepping walk which was perfect for Buck.

"Nice horse, Early," Custer nodded at Buck.

Yes, sir, I like her. She's as good a horse as a man could want."

A whitetail buck with a big rack jumped out to their left and veered off through the pines ahead of them. The dogs took off in pursuit and both men gave chase. They pressed the deer hard and he swung around to the north and dropped into heavy timber. The general's hounds pushed him up the opposite hill through the trees until the buck came out into a clear area heading for a swale in the hilltop.

Custer took aim so Early held back. The Remington barked, the buck strained, then tumbled back down the hill into the clamoring dogs. Custer was jubilant. He sent the big buck back to camp on a mule with Bloody Knife and gave the scout instructions to return with the mule and to rejoin their party as soon as possible. Two Strike pulled in close, with the other mules, and stayed closed up.

"Good shot, sir."

"Thanks, Early. Didn't mean to hunt going out but we're still close enough to camp to send it back and we are supposed to be hunting."

Picking up the thread of their previous conversation, Early asked, "Is your sorrel a thoroughbred, sir?"

"Yes, he is, from Kentucky. I ride my other horse, Dandy, on the trail - but this is my hunting horse. There's nothing like Vic for the hunt. He's good with the dogs, too - it's in his blood, I guess. Since we need to make a showing with some game when we come back, I rode Vic."

"Yes, sir." Early pointed ahead a little to the left. "We'll cross into that valley. Should line us up for French Creek. Can Bloody Knife find us alright?"

Custer nodded. "He's a good tracker - you almost couldn't hide from him."

Where the hillsides were bare, the sun was hot, so they rode mostly in the shade of tall pines. Grasshoppers buzzed in front of them but nowhere were there as many as they had seen on the plains.

They rode to the head of French Creek and watered their stock. Fed by countless fresh water springs, the clear stream quickly grew in size as they continued down the valley. By late afternoon, Jim asked if the general would want to make camp and check the creek.

"Are we near the spot now, Early?"

"Near, sir. Probably wouldn't hurt to be a little upstream and work our way down, do you think?"

"Good. Two Strike, will you set up a camp here and get a fire started?"

Two Strike grunted assent.

All three picketed their horses and the mules to eat grass. Early pulled a mess kit from his saddle bag and brought the Winchester along. Custer held something small in his hand and brought his rifle. Both men had Colts and plenty of ammo.

"See what you can find, Early. I'll go above you a ways and catch trout for our supper. I brought a fly line and some hooks that should work with hoppers."

"Yes, sir. Watch for shiny spots in the water."

"Come and get me if it gets exciting." Custer walked away.

At sunset, Custer rejoined Early carrying a string of ten nice trout. "Look at this one, Mr. Early." Custer showed off a fifteen inch brightly colored rainbow.

"Nice. Take a look at this." Early unfolded a small paper that held a scattering of gold flakes. "Could make a living this way, sir, but I've got a hunch it's gonna be better than this. Just need to look a little more."

"That's good, Early. It's here alright. How did you do it?"

"Used half my mess kit like a gold pan. Scooped up sand from the bottom of the creek and swirled it about with a little water. Tipped the edge of the pan down, and rocking the pan, slopped the water and most of the sand out. The gold is heavy enough, it stays in the pan. Watch."

Early demonstrated and wound up with three more little flakes. "You have to realize, sir, that a regular gold pan would be much better. Beyond that, a sluice box like they had in California would yield riches, I'll bet. This little tiny pan is just a toy."

"Let's go eat trout like kings, Early, and try your riches game again in the morning."

Back at camp, Bloody Knife was back, the fire was hot, and Two Strike had set up two A-tents for the white men.

After supper, the scouts talked together in Ree for a while and then walked out in different directions into the trees and lay down to sleep on grassy spots. Early stoked up the fire and sat with his back against a tree.

"Excellent trout, sir. Why don't you grab a few winks and I'll keep an eye out for a while?"

"Sounds good. Can you stay awake?"

"Sure, general, this was an easy day." Early sat by the fire until the other three seemed asleep. He could hear the horses and mules moving and the sound of the creek. As the moon came up, he decided to run a recon.

Early made a circle around the camp and looked around from a high bluff above French Creek. He didn't see anything suspicious. Then he heard a small sound behind him. Jim squatted and pivoted with the Colt in his fist, immediately facing the other way.

"Early, don't shoot."

"Two Strike, where the hell did you come from?"

Two Strike grinned. "You pretty good scout, Early. Me too."

"You sure are. Why aren't you sleeping?"

"Can't sleep. Want talk."

"What about?"

"You and Yellow Hair look for gold?"

"Yes. Don't tell."

"You my brother. Bloody Knife Pahuska's brother. No tell. We help when sun comes up."

"I'll clear it with the general. You think we're safe here?"

"Safe. No Sioux here. No whites here."

"I think so, too. Let's go grab some sleep."

"Shut eye." Two Strike smiled faintly.

"You bet." Early grinned and led the way back to camp. Most of the time he couldn't tell Two Strike was behind him. Pretty good scout.

Jim kept the fire up and slept off and on with his back to the tree. He could tell the others were all half awake, too. He made coffee when the sun hit the treetops.

FORTY SIX

"GENERAL, DID YOU BRING the Rees along with us for a reason?"

"Two reasons, Mr. Early - they're both good shots and we can trust them."

"With the gold story?"

"Yes. We'll split up today and look for gold. Show them what to do and we'll all prospect - that's all we'll all do today. You and I'll give each of them half a mess kit for a pan. Show them how you saved the gold. The indians have no interest in gold - we can trust them."

"When do we go back to the big camp?"

"Today is all the time we can spare for gold discovery - it's enough, though. We can cover a lot of creek in one whole day. We'll head back, hunting, at daybreak tomorrow. We'll need to load out those mules for our hunting story to be believable."

"Yes, sir." Early motioned to the Ree scouts to follow him. Custer gave half his mess kit to Bloody Knife. Jim showed them what to do and gave half his kit to Two Strike. He sent the indians together half a mile down the creek, Custer went upstream, and Early stayed where he had been the evening before.

Early took off his moccasins and his pants and rolled up his sleeves. He got right out into the cold stream and worked his pan. Colors showed up in almost every pan and his little store of dust grew magically. No nuggets, though.

At noon, Custer came into camp very excited. Custer had less dust but he had a small nugget about the size of the one Early had originally found. The Rees didn't come in. The two men had jerky and coffee and went together to check on their scouts. Jim brought some jerky along for them.

"See, Early," Two Strike said proudly. The indian scouts had a small piece of deerskin with their treasure heaped on it. They had three times as much gold as Custer and twice as much as Early and Custer put together. The Rees had three nuggets, one larger than any of the others.

"Show me how you did it," Custer said.

There was a high bank along the creek here, freshly caved off. Grass and plant roots hung out in the air - at eye level if you stood on the stream bed. Bloody Knife probed the black dirt and roots with his knife and let the loose dirt fall in his pan. He carefully slopped in a little water and expertly worked his pan. Gold dust glittered when he handed the wet pan to Custer.

"Look at that, gold in the grass roots," Custer exclaimed.

They all sat down on rocks in the hot sun and the Rees ate their lunch. Custer was dazed. For a long time, no one said anything.

"Significant findings, sir?" Early finally asked. "Yes, Early, just what your government and your country needs. Don't know how they'll work out the politics with the Sioux - but they will, somehow - when my report and this dust reach high command."

"There's no reason to leave the Black Hills lay here. The Sioux obviously use this area very little." Custer gathered all the dust and nuggets in the soft deerskin, pulled the top together and tied it tightly shut with a leather string. He jumped to his feet. "Let's shoot some deer and go home!"

In late afternoon, they began encountering small herds of deer coming out of the shelter of the trees onto the open meadows and valleys to feed. They arrived back at camp at ten o'clock, with the mules and the Ree's ponies loaded with ten deer.

After three long days with short nights, Early was quick to respond to Custer's summons early the next morning.

"Two full month's pay, Mr. Early - with horse allowance. I wish you well - you have my undying gratitude."

"Thank you, sir." The two shook hands. An hour later, Jim had his gear together and was up on Buck. He paused, watching two cavalry companies and the scientific corps leave with Custer in command. They were off to visit last year's battlefield where Captain O'Meara had made his stand, to bury whatever remains were there and to prepare a report for General Sheridan. They would also push out east into the badlands for geologic and paleontologic observations. Grant stayed in camp again - because the whiskey's here, Early thought.No one else knew about Rose and the bear except Grant, and Jim was sure no one ever would.

Jim shook the reins on Buck's neck and made a clicking sound and headed his horse west along the creek until he was out of sight of the command. Then, he crossed the creek and headed north.

FORTY SEVEN

THE CHEYENNE HUNTING PARTY returned to their big village with many travois loaded with buffalo meat and hides. They had plenty to sustain them on their trek to the Powder River. This had been a very successful hunt, another good omen for the future.

For days now, old men had kept a vigil on a hump in the prairie, north of the village, where they could watch for the hunters' return from the east. They had been the first to see the dust cloud far off and they had patiently watched as the young men rode closer and became recognizable. They were the first to approach the men coming into camp.

Women and young boys and girls were running between the lodges to meet the returning hunters. Old women stood just outside their lodges savoring the excitement. The village was ready for a great pow-wow and feasting to celebrate the successful hunt. All could see the heavily loaded travois and savored thoughts of fresh roasted buffalo hump.

Whirlwind Horse rode in on his paint pony, tired but at peace. He became uneasy, however, as he entered the village and couldn't see his wives anywhere among the milling crowd. As he turned his pony out, a frightful wailing came to his ears from inside his lodge. It sounded like mourning. Alarmed, he ducked into the teepee.

Screams and wails grew instantly louder as he appeared. His wives had tears streaming down their faces, their eyes were red and their faces were swollen from their grieving. He could see White Eagle was not here, but it was some time before Whirlwind could get the story from the women.

Whirlwind Horse staggered outside holding his head with both hands. He ran along the swift river until he fell to the ground in exhaustion, sobbing his breath in ragged gasps, his chest bursting.

After dark, he went back to his lodge and prayed silently with the pipe until he fell asleep on his back rest. His wives lay down on each side of him and slept with their heads on his lap and legs.

At the council of the chiefs the next morning, as the pipe was passed in deliberation, final plans were made to break camp and start for the Powder River country in a few days. In his turn, Whirlwind Horse spoke that he was going after the Bear God in Paha Sapa and that his wives would trail with the village on their journey. He would catch up in a few days so they should leave as planned and not wait for him. The old ones, the principal chiefs, agreed. All around the circle the rest grunted agreement.

Immediately after the meeting of the chief's council, the town crier rode around the village passing the news - both of moving the camp and of Whirlwind Horse's vow to kill the Bear God. All the people quickly knew of the council's decisions. Everyone knew the Whirlwind was brave and a good fighter and had strong medicine - no one would have liked to take his place in his pursuit of the Bear God. Still, they understood his deep feelings of the loss of his only son and his desire for revenge.

White Bull made up a special medicine for Whirlwind Horse to keep him safe from the powerful Bear God. White Bull prayed to the Great Power as he held the pipe out at arm's length, raised to the sky above. Occasionally, during his chant, he would lower the pipe to touch Whirlwind's head as the war chief knelt before him.

A sweat lodge was prepared on a hill away from the village. On a small mound of earth outside the entrance was placed a large, white buffalo skull. Whirlwind Horse pledged a piece of skin cut from each arm to be offered prayerfully, as a sacrifice, to obtain the courage and strength necessary to accomplish his purpose.

When the sun was high in the sky, Whirlwind Horse approached the sweat lodge, clad only in his breech clout. White Bull took a piece of charcoal from the sweat lodge fire and marked the war chief's upper arms. He then cut the skin from those places with the sharp edge of a flint arrow point. As he cut each piece off, he held it toward the sun, and with a prayer, placed the skin under the buffalo skull.

With blood running down his arms, Whirlwind Horse stoically did not cry out or flinch. He raised his arms to the sky and stared at the sun until there was a large black spot on it, praying silently for strength and safety. As he lowered his arms, White Bull guided him to the entrance of the sweat lodge. Whirlwind Horse dropped his breech clout outside and, naked, entered the smoky, hot interior.

For three days and nights, Whirlwind Horse prayed without sleeping and without eating or drinking. He sweat until he could sweat no more.

Before dawn on the fourth day, he had a vision that the fierce face of the bear appeared on the surface of the sun. As he watched, the bear became the black spot and darkness fell upon the earth. A bear's paw fell to the ground. The spot faded and as the light brightened, Whirlwind Horse rode out of the sun on his white war pony, shining bright as the sun, and descended toward his village once more.

As the apparition neared earth, Whirlwind noticed blood was pouring off his own body onto his horse. The color red was the life color and he felt the great joy of victory over the Bear God. Whirlwind Horse fell unconscious and White Bull dragged him from the sweat lodge.

When his eyes opened, White Bull offered the war chief sips from the water dipper. As he slowly began to move, the medicine man gave him dried buffalo meat to chew. By the time the sun came up, the Whirlwind had regained some strength. He picked up his breech clout and walked naked beside White Bull back to his own lodge.

The big village was gone, leaving a wide trail to the west clearly marking their departure. Whirlwind Horse entered his lodge. All of his personal needs were left for him here. He lay down on his sleeping robes and immediately went into a deep sleep, oblivious to his surroundings.

When he awoke the next morning, the sun was warming the teepee and White Bull was gone. He could hear his war pony outside the lodge. He ate some more dried buffalo.

He painted his face and body with broad crimson marks as if for war, and pulled on his horsehide pants, to protect his legs riding in brush, and his moccasins. He painted red circles around the eyes of his white pony. With his Henry and knife, food and ammo, and White Bull's medicine bag, Whirlwind Horse rode to the swift river.

He watered his horse and washed off the blood from his arm cuts. He drank from the stream and filled a U.S. canteen he had taken after the battle. Crossing the stream, he found the bear's tracks where it had carried off the baby.

It was a sunny day with a light breeze and Whirlwind felt alert and especially ready to fight the great bear to the finish. He watched the ground carefully for an occasional track as he rode away from the swift river. With his rifle laid across the saddle pad, he was ready for action.

He came to a piece of soft, tanned deerskin with blood on it at a spot where several big bear tracks showed. There was blood on the grass nearby. Whirlwind Horse screamed an anguished cry and then a long, loud war cry. He kicked his pony's ribs and scrambled up the mountain brandishing his "yellow boy" rifle at arm's length above his head.

When he reached the hilltop, he couldn't find any tracks. He headed west and found sign again. He found a few bear tracks off and on until he came to the bones of the cavalry horse that had obviously been eaten by the bear. There was enough withered hide sticking to bones so he could identify it. Whirlwind remembered that horse being lost from the pony herd in a blizzard last winter.

Here, bear sign was plentiful. Whirlwind even found the bear's bed where it had lain to guard the horse carcass as he rested during the time he ate here - but all this sign was old.

The war chief rode circles and could tell the bear had spent considerable time in the general area. Whirlwind Horse hunted for days in ever-widening circles with stops on ridges and peaks where he could see big country while he rested. O'Meara's field glass helped him see into brushy spots and into the shade under trees. The Bear God, even any fresh tracks, eluded him. Revenge burned in his belly like a glowing coal. He was very frustrated and anxious. He became nervous and couldn't stop moving. He was driven from first light to dark every day by his unending need to find the Bear God.

One day, as he rode along a ridge, he thought he saw the bear. In a glance, he noticed a flash of brown about a mile away as it moved quickly through a small clearing in the valley below. Whirlwind Horse was now rock steady as he hurried his pony toward the clearing. Rifle in hand as he moved through the valley, he came to fresh tracks in a wet spot. The war chief paused and was awed by the size of that track and the span of the gait where the big animal had run through. The light wind was blowing up the valley in his favor. The bear track angled up the next hillside into thick trees and brush.

Whirlwind Horse skirted the timber on the open, rocky slope. The bear walked out into the open on the hillside above him, grazing. He pulled the walking pony to a stop and brought the Henry to his shoulder.

As Whirlwind Horse squeezed off a shot, his pony moved. Up the hill, at the same time, the giant grizzly roared and stood upright. The bear immediately dropped to all fours and, running for the timber, turned his head and snapped repeatedly at his hind leg.

Whirlwind Horse held back, waiting to see what the bear might do. As he approached the timber slowly, watching the ground and watching for the bear, he thought he saw blood on the grass.

The grizzly stood up from his bed behind a bush and the white pony exploded, screaming in fear. The pony dumped Whirlwind to the ground and ran down the hillside. As he was bucked off, Whirlwind's body twisted in the air. He lost his grip on his rifle and it flew and smashed onto a big rock.

Hitting the ground knocked the wind out of Whirlwind Horse but he knew the danger he was in. Gasping for breath and fighting pain and unconsciousness, Whirlwind got his legs under him and dove for his Henry. Whirling, the Cheyenne brought the rifle up, pointed it at the charging bear, and tried to pull the trigger.The brass receiver on the Henry was bent from the impact of hitting the rock and wouldn't fire.

Whirlwind Horse screamed as the grizzly went for his throat. He pounded on the bear's huge face with the broken rifle, but the grizzly clamped his jaws down on Whirlwind's right arm. Blood spurted. The bone snapped and he dropped the rifle.

In agony, the powerful man fought bravely. He stabbed the bear's paw with his knife and sawed, severing some tendons. The bear roared. He stabbed the bear's throat and cut his face as the bear mauled and bit him with terrible savagery.

In the end, he was no match for the Bear God.

The severely wounded grizzly left the dead chief's body and moved into the timber.

FORTY EIGHT

AFTER LEAVING THE COMMAND, Jim Early rode through the mountainous country north of Custer's camp. He soon encountered granite spires and boulders which made travel impossible. Travelling northwest, he left the solid rock behind, and passed north of Castle Creek valley. He rode the ridges, up the peaks, and through the valleys searching for the grizzly.

Days passed. From time to time he crossed old bear tracks. Some were the sign of the one he sought, but sometimes they were of smaller grizzlies or black bears.

Many days went by without seeing any bear at all or any fresh tracks. Other kinds of wild game were plentiful but Early didn't want to spook his prey by shooting. He ate jerky carried from the army camp. Berries of several types were abundant, especially raspberries. Large service berries hung in thick clusters bending down their branches. There were some blackberries, wild strawberries, and many wild cherries. Cold, fresh-water streams were in almost every valley, bounding down from springs on the hillsides.

Jim was sitting on a ridge, letting Buck graze nearby, when he noticed movement along the tree line at the edge of a burn. Early glassed the spot for a closer look. When he focused in on the movement, he was looking at a sow grizzly and two cubs carding raspberries with their long curved claws. As he watched, one of the cubs ran after a woodchuck until it holed up. The mother bear dug it out, with her big front feet throwing an avalanche of dirt and rocks, until she had the unfortunate small animal clamped between her jaws.

Jim rode out to the north rim where he could look over the

foothills to the prairie beyond. He then coursed south and west, and back north, in a zigzag pattern. Travelling west one day, he came to a very deep, wide canyon with steep canyon walls, impassible from these heights. He looked down on a pretty fair stream plunging to the north, a small river.

He rode north along the canyon rim until he could see a separate line of hills north of the Black Hills proper with a wide rolling plain in between. The river came out of the canyon and flowed through the valley. A single teepee was near the stream.

Early dismounted and glassed the teepee. There had been a big village here that had recently pulled out leaving a wide trail to the west. Custer's expedition had passed west of here a couple weeks ago and had not crossed the indian trail, so the movement was very recent. He thought this had probably been the Cheyenne camp and they had wintered here. He put his field glass away and rode east along part of the ridge he had already passed south of. Suddenly, he pulled Buck around and rode in a small circle. He stopped her as he saw what he had been looking for. In a deer trail leading through a patch of quaking aspen, there were fresh bear tracks. Without dismounting he could see the track with the missing toe, heading east ahead of him. The big grizzly was easy to follow here. About a mile later, the tracks were joined by those of an unshod horse. A pony had come from the north, gone west and then back east along this same rim. As he continued east, he lost the easy tracks but every once in a while he came upon sign of the bear and, from time to time, he would also see the horse tracks.

Jim crossed over to the next ridge south, and back and forth, finding plenty of bear sign, some old, some new. Also, he saw many horse tracks crossing and following the bear sign, all fresh. This was no loose horse.

This seemed to be an indian looking for the big grizzly and he was ahead of Early. He thought it was unusual that an indian would go out of his way to run into a big bear ... maybe ... a Cheyenne might.

Early shut down at dark. He couldn't follow the trail without light. He didn't build a fire and he saw no trace of any fire anywhere as he scouted the surrounding country from the high north ridge.

Early slept very little, and when he did, he had nightmares about the damned bear and Rose.

At first light, Early was leading Buck, watching the ground closely. As it got lighter, he mounted up. He lost the bear. He saw where the pony went off south into a valley. Horse droppings were fresh from the day before. Early rode on east for a mile or so but only saw fresh deer sign. Not likely a bear was here yesterday or last night. He rode back to the pony trail and urged Buck off the ridge to the south.

It was harder to track in the grassy valley but sometimes he would see broken grass, places where the grass was matted down, or a broken twig. He rode slowly looking for any confirming clue.

A shot rang out ahead of Jim and echoed through the canyons. He whoaed Buck. Only silence, no more shots. One shot was all. Jim took his bearings and rode at a canter down the valley, throwing caution to the wind. His bear was up ahead somewhere and so was someone else. One thing at a time.

Early pulled up. A flash of white caught his eye - ahead and up to his right. A white pony ran down the hill to the valley, then stopped and looked back at where he came from. The pony looked familiar. Red rings around his eyes ... could only belong to Whirlwind Horse and this pony was painted for war. Nothing made sense.

Jim walked Buck ahead watching the hillside above. They spooked the pony. It flared out across the valley and circled west.

Early walked Buck up the hill where the pony had come down until he got to the edge of the heavy pine growth. Jim left his horse and walked up the hill along the edge of the timber. Buck stood nervously, shied, trotted down to the valley and stood facing back uphill.

Jim stopped, aghast at the sight of the dead chief sprawled out on the ground, covered with blood. That damned grizzly did get Whirlwind Horse! Memory of the rain-soaked vale where this bear killed Rose washed over Early. Momentarily, he stood stunned.

The danger of his situation brought Early back to his senses. Within his grasp was the end of his long search. He systematically surveyed the kill scene. He saw the rifle. He could hardly drag his eyes away from the Cheyenne's broken, bloody body - he was painted for war! Jim was sure there was no other indian here and this one was no longer a threat ... but the bear might still be just a few feet away in the trees. The grizzly had not fed on the body. Why? Maybe because it had heard Early coming and was waiting for him. Maybe because it was wounded and was trying to move away from the hurt.

Jim saw the blood on the grass away from the body. Couldn't be the indian's. There was plenty of blood around the body but Early could see the extent of the struggle and this blood was out farther from the trees. Jim walked slowly toward the bloody grass, never taking his eyes off the trees, the Winchester at the ready. Eery silence prevailed.

There was a clot of something in the grass beside the bloody spot and Early could see a blood trail going to the woods. Jim picked up the clot - coarse, bloody brown hair! Whirlwind Horse had connected.

Early moved in close to the body, constantly watching the trees, rifle ready. He glanced down and saw the Whirlwind's knife. It was covered with blood, there was bear hair and flesh on the blade. He had stuck the bear as he was dying! Then, Early saw blood spots leading into the trees. Early's obsession forced him to follow the bear's path.

He found where the grizzly had lain. There was another pool of blood on the ground, and a few drops heading up the hill from the bed. Jim's quarry was leaving, getting away ... and he was close to it.

Early hurried down the hill and caught his horse. As he rode back up the hill, he swung wide around the kill scene, rode to the mountain top and left Buck where she wouldn't smell the bear or the blood. Jim dropped the bridle to the ground and unsaddled her. He rubbed her neck as he walked away. She would stay close.

FORTY NINE

EARLY FOUND THE BLOOD trail where the grizzly had crossed the top going south. The bear was travelling in a straight line across open country ... until, at the crest of another hill, the bear entered thick, brushy timber.

Jim started to skirt the woods. Looking ahead, he saw the bear standing in the open. The grizzly swung its huge head toward Early and he couldn't believe its face seemed to be all silver. He took a fine sight with the Winchester. Though it was big, the bear was a small target from this distance, he held a little high. As Early fired, the bear jumped but didn't fall. It ran into the trees.

Jim's heart raced. He half ran across the space to where the bear had been standing. Sure enough, there was blood spattered on a rock. He hadn't missed! From such a distance, it was impossible to pinpoint the shot - maybe he was lucky to even hit his target. It was a long reach.

Early paused to steady down. Very large raindrops started to fall. He looked up at huge black rain clouds boiling overhead. They seemed to be moving in a circular pattern directly above him and rolling at the same time. Angry looking sky.

Thunder boomed in a long roll, lightning stabbed through the clouds at the horizon. Just like when Rose was killed. Rain started to pour as he walked slowly into the timber.

The bear's trail of blood drops led through big trees to a small clearing. A large juniper bush, tall and fifteen feet across, was near the right edge of the clearing and the blood trail seemed to go directly to the juniper.

Under the trees, the rain was broken up by the branches above, so the blood drops still showed plainly on the ground. In the clearing, the sheet of water poured down full strength. Jim couldn't see any sign beyond the juniper but it might be washed away. He still couldn't see the bear.

He slipped on wet pine needles but saved himself from falling by reaching out to a twenty feet high rock formation near his right hand. His rifle stock banged the rock. He quickly regained his footing and moved just one step at a time, trying to see behind the juniper on his left, rifle ready.

He took another step. Water was pouring off his hat brim and washing down his face. He kept blinking to be able to see. As he took another step, he could see behind the juniper.

The grizzly charged from behind the rock and knocked Early out into the clearing, face down in the mud. As he lost the Winchester, he pulled the trigger and it fired in the air.

Early came up on his hands and knees with the rifle just beyond his reach. The bear's great jaws clamped down on his buttock. The enraged grizzly was growling, shaking Jim's body like a rag doll, and biting.

Pain raged through Early's body and he was nearly unconscious. He fought to revive. His body momentarily relaxed and the bear released his hold.

Early lunged for the rifle but his huge antagonist bit all the way through his leg above the knee and held him in place. Early passed out. The bear pulled away.

When he came to, he moved slightly and the bear attacked. Jim was covered with blood and the grizzly was biting him again and again. He got the Colt in his right hand and passed out.

He was unconscious for minutes. Jim opened his eyes slowly. He saw the bear was watching him from about ten feet away, ears laid back. He was careful not to twitch as he assessed his situation. Mercifully, the pain was much less, his senses weren't relaying to the brain anymore. The monster's unearthly appearance was caused by the silver grizzled hairs entirely covering its face and from its unbelievable size. This evil presence seemed to be the devil himself on earth!

The grizzly roared as he charged straight for Jim's throat. Early pointed the Colt dead center in the huge, open mouth and pulled the trigger. The .44 blew a hole out the back of the head and bear brains, blood, and bone sprayed across the clearing.

Early rolled to the side and the two thousand pound body fell short of falling on him. The giant carcass slid in the mud, settled with a great sigh, and lay still. Jim passed out.

Miles away, Two Strike was one of the scouts leading Custer's 7th out of the north side of the Black Hills. He was alone. He heard the first shot as he topped a ridge and he was listening intently when the second shot echoed across the mountains.

Had to be his brother Early, he thought. No one from the expedition was west of the indian scouts. He had a feeling Early needed his help, so he headed toward where he thought the sounds had come from. Two Strike wiped the water from his face as he rode. The rain had stopped.

Early lay on his back in the clearing, blood soaked, deep bite wounds covering his body. He looked up at the sky - looked like a whirlpool in the clouds with the center straight above him. The dark clouds whirled around a light spot that was growing larger.

Bright sunlight broke through the light spot, individual rays shining down through the trees. One ray lighted up Early's face. It seemed so peaceful now. He felt glad that he had killed the grizzly for Rose. The rain was over. The pain was gone.

Somehow, he felt the presence of his brother, Two Strike, approaching. That was good. He could count on Two Strike to take care of everything.

The light ray flickered on Jim's face. "I'm coming," Jim said.